about the author

Anne Bailey was born in Woking in 1958 and went to school in Surrey. She has tried a variety of jobs, including farm and factory work, and has spent a short time on a kibbutz in Israel.

She always wanted to write, but her first book, *Scars* was not published until 1987, but was quickly followed by *Burn Up* and *Rhythm and Blues* and, recently, *Israel's Babe*. Her other interests are music, films and reading about psychiatry. She lives in a mobile home in Surrey and has her own transport — a Kawasaki 200cc motorbike.

SCARS
Anne Bailey

faber and faber
LONDON · BOSTON

First published in Great Britain in 1987
by Faber and Faber Limited
3 Queen Square London WC1N 3AU

This paperback edition first published in 1991

Printed in England by Clays Ltd, St Ives plc

A CIP record for this book is available from the British Library.

ISBN: 0-571-16322-x

To Mum,
for helping me through the bad times

Chapter One

He was there. He was always there in my mind. A great lumbering shadow. I couldn't do anything or say anything without remembering. I hadn't spoken since it happened. I couldn't speak. Even to do so would defy all my morals. My honesty.

I spent some time in a special hospital. They sent me to a special school. All the while the court case was going on. All the while my mother was dissolving their marriage. She'd tell me, so softly, so softly, that we were rid of him. When he was sentenced I laughed. But still I couldn't talk. And I hated men. I hated every man except my brother. He was the only male I loved. He would always be the only man I loved.

We settled into a life of normality. Mum, Jason and I. Everything was over and done with. Finished. But still I couldn't speak.

I was fourteen when it happened. I was sixteen when Mum told me she was going to marry again. It had been on the cards, of course. It was an old family friend who lived in Kent. He was a vet. Somehow his being a professional person made things seem worse for me. He seemed so much better than me. Better. Cleaner. It was his goodness against my badness. My own badness which I couldn't escape from. Good against bad. Him against me. I just couldn't get near him.

"We're getting married," Mum said, holding my hands. "That's what we've decided."

I looked down. To the fawn carpet. But no carpet was within my sight. No carpet. Just a hole.

Mum cupped her hands over my cheeks. "We'll move to Kent," she said. "Away from here. To where Gerry lives. His house is big enough for us all. You'll like it there, Tanya. Away from all this."

I held my breath. Screwed my eyes tightly shut. I honestly believe I wanted to die. Sometimes it seemed the only way out.

"Stop that, Tanya!" Mum shouted. "At once. Stop it. We don't have tantrums."

Her words meant nothing. I wanted to die.

"Stop it, I said. Now."

I didn't stop it. She slapped me round the face and I breathed again.

"Now, you listen to me." She was angry. "You listen. None of us are going to live in the past for ever. We're going to make a future for ourselves. We have to. I love Gerry, Tanya. He loves me. He's the best man I've ever met. We're both prepared to make a go of it. For us. For our children. So you've got to accept it, Tanya. For my sake if not for yours. Dr Smart knows everything. You'll be transferred to another doctor in Kent, so you've got nothing to worry about. Nothing at all. But I'm not going to be blackmailed by you and your tantrums. I won't have them. And if you carry on like that I'll get Dr Smart to give you an injection."

I shook my head; violently.

"Well, just do as I say then."

She moved away from me. I went after her. Grabbing her arms. Pulling her to me. I hated her to be

2

angry with me. I needed her so much.

"Well, you know when you make me cross," she said, wrapping her arms around me. "I just can't cope with you sometimes. I love Gerry, Tanya. I need him. Try to understand that."

I had to understand, didn't I? There was nothing else for me to do. How I lay awake at night, though. Thinking and thinking. Of living with another man. Wishing and wishing. That maybe Mum would one day say it was all off. Maybe. Maybe. Maybe. How great it would be. I was scared, you see. Scared of men. It brought it all back. The day. The time. The action. There was nothing good in a man. Nothing at all.

Mum never said it was off and the date was set. October twelfth. At our local church. Just two months away. I grew moody around the house. I'd sit alone in my bedroom for hours upon hours. All day. All night. Trying to think of a way to escape. Gerry came and brought his children. A boy of fourteen and girl of seventeen. I locked myself in my room. Pretending they weren't there. But I could hear them laugh downstairs. Laughing and talking. I felt terribly lonely. Exiled. I punched my bed. Bit my clenched fists.

Chapter Two

"Are you angry?" Dr Smart said.

I just stared ahead of me.

"I haven't done anything to you. Why're you angry with me?"

YOU WANT THEM TO MARRY, I wrote on my notepad.

"Yes. I think it will make you all very happy."

NOT ME.

"How can you be so sure?"

I KNOW.

"I know why you don't want them to marry. Because the thought of living with another father figure makes you sick, doesn't it?"

I didn't answer.

"Because you think every man is going to be like your father."

YOU'RE A MAN.

"Well done. But you only see me for fifteen minutes a fortnight. You're going to be living with Gerry."

SO?

"So? What? You tell me. You're the one who's angry."

HE BELIEVES IN GOD. HE GOES TO CHURCH. I DON'T BELIEVE IN GOD.

He laughed. "Now that is a feeble excuse."

DON'T LAUGH AT ME.

"Why? Are you so fragile? No I don't think so. I think you kid us sometimes. To get just what you want."

I looked down at my fingers.

"When you've become bored with the game you might start talking."

I savagely pushed my notepad from the desk.

"Well, you have to do some work. You can't expect us to do it all for you."

I began to write on the desk until he took the pen away from me.

"What happened on that day, Tanya? Can you remember?"

I shook my head.

"Why won't you talk, then? We all know the truth."

I left the room. Slamming the door. It was the last time I should see him. I didn't care. It didn't matter. He hadn't helped me, anyway. But I cried. I cried just a bit as I ran to my bus stop.

It was on a Monday. The wedding. At three o'clock in the afternoon. There were a lot of people there. The church was full. I sat at the front. In a row next to Jason and my Gran. His son and daughter were there too. It was meant to be a happy occasion. But I wasn't happy. I hated being inside the church. I felt as if I didn't belong there. Not me, not the way I was. I felt so damn ugly.

The marriage ceremony took about three-quarters of an hour. There were readings and a woman singing a solo. I just stared at the hymn book in front of me and took no part in the service. I didn't even stand when the others stood. I didn't kneel when

5

they knelt. The whole affair was beyond me. I knew that after the reception in a hotel Mum was going to drive me and Jason to Kent. To his house. With just two packed cases of our belongings. It wasn't until the following Tuesday that a removal van was going to take the rest of our stuff over. I kept thinking of that during the service. That we'd be going to live with Gerry. It made me feel gut-sick.

The reception was at a hotel in a place I didn't really know. I'd never been there before. In Halford.

"Hello, Tanya. D'you want a sherry?" His daughter. Sarah was her name. She came over to me, when we were in the hotel. Following her was a waitress with a tray of sherries. "Take a sherry."

In one swoop I'd knocked the tray out of her hands. I was aware of the commotion that followed. I stalked out. Aware of all the eyes upon me. I stalked out of the hotel. Along a driveway and out on to a main road which was busy with traffic. I just had to get away. So I walked as quickly as I could, mixing with all the crowds. Walking. I walked. I walked. Escaping. All the time escaping.

I stopped. Somewhere along the street. I just stopped. Drained of all my anger. I was scared to be alone with so many strange people. In a place I didn't know. I was scared that Mum would be cross with me. I suddenly felt guilty and selfish. Awfully selfish. It was Mum's day. Mum's big day and I must have spoilt it all. I cried there on the street. I turned back and began retracing my footsteps. Half an hour later I was back at the hotel. I couldn't face going in, so sat on a wooden seat at the front of the hotel. I must have been there for another half an hour when Jason came out of the front entrance. He looked very smart in his new suit. He sat next to me.

"Nothing's spoilt," he said. "You've missed the meal, though."

I was relieved. His words comforted me. Nothing's spoilt. Jason understood. Everything he understood.

"They're going to open some of their presents. Are you coming in?"

I was afraid of all those eyes that would be upon me.

"Come on." He took my hand. "Come on."

It wasn't so bad. The hall was full of gay chatter. Jason took me to the wedding table and sat down next to me. Piles of presents were in front of us. Gerry and Mum were opening them together. Smiling. Laughing. Thanking.

Jason turned and smiled at me.

I smiled back.

He passed another present to Gerry.

Chapter Three

The sun was still shining when we were on our way to Gerry's house. Out of Surrey. Into Kent. I don't know why the sun was shining. It sort of mocked me. Mock. Mock. Mock. You're going to live with Gerry. Ha. Ha. Ha. And so the story went.

I was tired. It had been a long day. I felt tense and irritable. Mum was following Gerry to his house. I wondered what my room would be like.

"Here we are then," Mum said. Stopping the car beside Gerry's. Sarah and Clive were already out. Sarah opened Mum's car door.

"You didn't burn him up, Kath. You could have taken him easily."

"I didn't want to ruin his ego so soon."

They both laughed. There was banging of more doors. Talking. Shouting. I just sat there. Not being sure what to do. I was alone in the car. Alone with my thoughts. All men are monsters. They're dark, evil. All men are Satan. Ugly. Satan.

"Tanya." Mum opened the door. "Come on. We're going in. I'll give you your tablets, then you'd better get to bed."

I followed her into the kitchen. It was a very tall kitchen with a wooden table running along the middle of it.

"What would you like to drink, Tanya?" Gerry asked.

I said nothing.

"She's got to take her tablets," Mum said. "I'll get her some water."

"Jason! Clive! Sarah!" Gerry shouted. "What d'you want to drink?"

"Here you are, love." Mum gave me my tablets with a glass of water. They were tranquillizers and anti-depressant tablets.

"Have we got any Coke, Dad?"

"I'll have coffee."

"There's Coke in the fridge, love. Jason?"

"Coffee, please. Two sugars, no milk."

"As if I don't remember."

"You don't even remember how I like my coffee, Dad," Sarah said.

"Just because you change it every five minutes."

"No, I don't. Do I, Kath?"

"Hey, don't bring me into your arguments."

"Not yet anyway," Gerry said. "Let her settle in first, Sarah."

"Are there any straws, Dad?"

"I can't do a hundred things at once. Find them yourself."

"I'll get them," Mum said. "Straws? Straws? Now let me take a guess at it."

"Larder."

"Thank you, darling. Straws. Here you are. Sarah."

"Thank you."

"I'll take Tanya and show her the room," Mum said. "Come on, Tanya."

I went with her. Up a large oak staircase. Along a short corridor.

"That's the bathroom," Mum said. "And along here, here is your bedroom." She opened the door. I went in. It was quite bare. A bed. A chest of drawers. The wallpaper was old-fashioned.

"We're going to decorate it exactly how you want it," Mum said. "When you get your own things in here it'll look more like home."

I went to the window. It was quite a large room with bay window-sills. It looked out on to fields. Land.

"Well?" Mum said. "You like it?"

I nodded. To please her. Not too convinced, though.

My suitcase was on the bed. Mum opened it and took my washing gear out. "You go along to the bathroom and have a wash. I'll find your nightie."

I did as she said. I felt a stranger, though, in the bathroom. It seemed to belong to another family. Another family which I wasn't a part of.

Mum was ready with my nightie when I arrived back to my room. She'd put the suitcase on the floor. I changed in front of her and was already beginning to feel sleepy because of the strong tablets.

Mum saw me into bed and sat on the edge, holding my hand.

"D'you want your notepad?"

Just in case I wanted to tell her something. I usually did when she sat on my bed at night. We used to have fun together. But I shook my head then. I didn't feel like having fun. Perhaps I never would again.

"All right, love, you just get to sleep. I'll pop in later." She kissed me on the head. "I'll leave your door open a bit. God bless, darling."

I listened. I listened to all the strange noises of this

10

house. This vet's surgery. Animals. Ghosts? Creaks and groans. I listened to the sound of talking. Far off. Far off. I heard a man's voice but didn't really know who it belonged to. The drugs made me sleep. I slept.

Chapter Four

First of all when I woke I wondered where I was. For a moment I thought I was back in hospital. It worried me, until I remembered. And when I remembered it seemed even worse than hospital. I looked at my watch to find the time was quarter past nine. The house was quiet. I heard nothing. I didn't want to go downstairs and bump into Gerry. I wanted him to be out, always out. Always far from me. I didn't want to get close enough for him to touch me. I remembered, you see. That monster. Lurking close, so close. And if he, Gerry, were to touch me. Were just to touch me, then it would bring it all back. I would have to remember then. Have to remember. That day. That day. Which seemed like yesterday.

"Get up, you lazy toad."

Jason made me jump.

"Come on. Get up." He began tickling me and we had a friendly fight.

"I'll get Mum to bring you a cup of tea."

I reached for my notepad. AREN'T YOU START-ING WORK TODAY?

"First day tomorrow. Gerry's taking me and Clive into town at ten. Clive's skived a day off school. He's going to show me around the place. We might go to the flicks even."

Jason had found a job in Cherryhurst when he'd

stayed with Gerry for a month. He'd landed a job in a supermarket.

"D'you want anything in town, Tanya?"

I shook my head.

"I might even get you a surprise prezzy. You never know your luck." He winked at me and ruffled my hair. "Right, I'll tell Mum you're awake," he said, bouncing out of my room. Bouncing. Bounce. Bounce. Bounce. He was happy. I could tell that. He was happy to be in this house. Happy to be starting a new job. I sighed. Perhaps wishing that I was that happy too. It seemed so warm and inviting. But then Jason didn't have the memories. Not the memories, which I did. Although he was four years older than me, he didn't have the memories.

Mum brought me a cup of tea soon after Jason went. She was on holiday from work for a week. She worked in a bank and she'd been transferred to a branch in Kent. She was still going to work. I don't think she could have been satisfied with just being a vet's wife.

"It's a lovely morning," Mum said, drawing back my curtains to show the blue sky. "Did you sleep all right?"

I nodded.

"D'you want a cooked breakfast?"

I wrote on my notepad:

I WANT BREAKFAST AT TEN.

"At ten?"

I nodded.

"All right. If that's what you want."

I nodded again.

"Be up and dressed for ten then. I'll see you down-stairs."

*

I waited until five past ten, when I could be sure that Jason and Gerry had left. Then I went gingerly downstairs. Scared that they might still be there.

Mum was in the kitchen and the breakfast smelt lovely. I sat at the table. Listening to the radio.

"I figured it out," Mum said.

I quizzed her with my eyes.

"Why you wanted to come down at ten."

I just shrugged. Who cared? It was only important to me.

"What're you going to do? Run upstairs every time he comes in? We're not at home in Surrey any more, you know."

I fiddled with the salt pot which was on the table.

"You're going to have to try, Tanya. I know it will be hard, but you can try. If you want to. He's not going to hurt you and you know it."

OK. OK. OK. I didn't want to listen. I wished I could turn her voice off like I could turn the radio off.

"Here. Eat your breakfast. D'you want some ketchup?"

I nodded.

She gave me it. Then she began to sing. She was happy. I was scared. Of any minute him coming through that door. She was happy. I was scared. She was happy. I was scared. She was singing. Happy. Not caring about my fear. I felt alone. Again. Isolated. The desert was around me. Barren. Empty. I thought it was empty. Until I saw that shadow. Still. Moving. Still. Coming for me. Nearer and nearer. Outside. In the desert. But there's a door in the desert and it was opening. He was coming in. I was alone with him. Mum had gone. Jason had gone. I was alone, wasn't I? Wasn't I? But the truth laughed at me. The truth was like an ugly, warted, sliding monster. Ready to eat me; eat me; eat me.

I pushed the empty plate away from me. The door stayed closed. I was still tense, though. Waiting. And still Mum was singing. And still her word, try, echoed in my mind.

"Sarah writes," Mum said. Out of the blue.

I looked at her.

"She's writing a book. I told her you like to write. You must get together. She works on a farm at the moment." I just listened.

"What are you going to do today, Tanya? We could walk to the village. Have a look around the shops. You'll want to join the library, won't you?"

I loved reading. It was my favourite hobby.

"I don't know what Gerry's got on his agenda for the day. Surgery's not until twelve. We'll have to wait until he gets back. Perhaps you could go up and make your bed now. I don't want you staying in that room, though. I want you down afterwards. Bring your notepad too."

I slowly made my bed. I sat on the window-sill for a while, looking down at the empty space of land. I had to go downstairs, though, or I knew Mum would be up. She's good to her word. I took my notepad and flicked through its pages. Conversations. Words. Poems. A part of my life. A large part. Because I couldn't talk. I could only write. It becomes like a habit, you see. Writing instead of talking. It becomes like a habit. I knew I couldn't talk, though. I knew I wouldn't talk. All because of that day. I knew. That day. So I wouldn't talk again; never.

*

Mum showed me to the large lounge, which seemed very stately to me. Large, old-fashioned-type furniture. Couch. Chairs. And leading off into a dining room which had a mahogany table and chairs in it. With a sideboard to match. I walked over to it. Studied the large framed photos of Clive and Sarah. Smiling; school photos. How happy. How sweet. Tra la la.

I sat and opened my notepad. I began doodling. Different shapes. Then I began writing.

I HATE GERRY. I HATE SARAH. I HATE CLIVE. I HATE HIM. HIM. HIM. HIM IS A MONSTER. HIM IS A CHILD. HIM IS A CAT GONE EVER SO WILD.

The door opened. Suddenly he was standing there. Quite short. Broad-shouldered. Dark-haired. Brown eyes. Suddenly he was standing there and I froze.

"Hello, Tanya. All right?"

I stared hard at the notepad in front of me.

"What've you been writing?" He walked over to look. I didn't care what he could see.

"I'll find the cat for you. She's probably up in Clive's room. I'll bring her down."

He did bring her down and put her on the settee next to me. She was tiny. A tabby and white kitten. I waited until he'd gone out of the room and then I began to stroke her. She was gorgeous. I could hear her purr. I patted my lap and she came on to it. Her nose touched mine. I loved her. She was so affectionate. In the end she curled up on my lap. I didn't dare move in case I disturbed her.

Mum came in and asked if I wanted a cup of coffee. She stroked Tiger and the cat jumped off my lap to follow her out.

16

"Come out to the kitchen, love. We'll have coffee in there."

It was like a marathon being run inside my body. Nerves trying to outbeat each other. Trying to run faster and faster. It made me breathless.

I sat at the kitchen table opposite Gerry. I looked down into my circling coffee and tried to pretend he wasn't there.

Mum and he were talking. I could hear their voices but couldn't take in the words. I was alienated from them. Something was between us. Stopping us from touching. A barrier. Which I just couldn't bring down.

"Are you coming with us, Tanya?"

I heard my name. It was a male voice.

"Tanya, Gerry's talking to you."

"We're taking a walk down the village. D'you want to come?"

"It'll do you good to get some fresh air."

I shook my head.

"You can join the library," Mum said.

I could have screamed. Although no sound would have come. No. No. No. Help. Help. Help. Leave me alone. Just me. Just me. Just me.

"All right. It doesn't matter. You can guard the house for us," Gerry said. "I'll be picking up a couple of magazines for the others. What do you like to read?"

For the first time I looked at him. I don't know why. It was just a reaction. I usually received a magazine called *Seventeen*. It came on Mondays, you see. I thought I wouldn't receive it again once we moved away.

"Write it." Gerry pushed my notepad along the table. "Any magazine. What d'you normally have?"

I looked at Mum.

"Go on, Tanya. Tell him."

I wrote it. Slowly. Very slowly.

SEVENTEEN.

There seemed to be a huge sigh of relief in the kitchen although I hadn't heard anything.

"Right. I'll remember that. And while we're out you can feed the cat. Don't worry about the phone if it rings. Just leave it."

I picked up my notepad and went back to the lounge. I felt I'd done something. Done something good. But then I chided myself. I hadn't done anything good. Because I couldn't. It wasn't possible. Not for me. Not after that. After what? I questioned myself. After what? And I wondered. I really did wonder. But no one lifted the curtain. No one had rehearsed Act Two.

Chapter Five

Wednesday I was alone for most of the day. Mum and Gerry had travelled to Surrey to supervise the removal people. I quite enjoyed myself. I played with Tiger for much of the time and sat with her curled up at my side on the settee. I felt at ease. There was no one to bother me. I had a look around the house. Tried to feel at home. And actually I had to admit to myself that it was a warm house. A warm atmosphere. Stately but warm.

When Clive arrived home from school and Jason from work I was still alone in the house.

Clive, tall, thin and fair-haired, came flying into the lounge and dumped his school books on the floor.

"Tiggy. Tiggy. Tiggy," he said, picking up the cat and stroking her. "Have you been playing with Tanya? You spoilt moggy, you."

He switched on the telly, flung off his tie and collapsed in a bedraggled heap on the floor in front of it. I watched his actions and funnily enough warmed to him. He was so gentle for a boy. He didn't pressurize me at all. I felt at ease with him. And he didn't try it on with me. He just sort of accepted me. Without question.

There was a cartoon programme on the telly and I grew quite interested in it. It was funny. I even managed to laugh. Once. Just once.

"It's good, isn't it?" Clive said.

I nodded.

"I didn't know you could laugh. I thought you couldn't make any sound at all." He turned to look at me.

I felt inclined to write on my notepad, so did.

I CAN LAUGH.

"Do you really want to talk?"

I nodded.

"Dad says there's no such thing as can't. It's either I want or I don't want."

I shrugged. Perhaps that was true. Perhaps I didn't want to talk. Why was that, though? Why? It all added up. All made sense to me. The reasons. The reasons. Which happened to be far away then. Far away. I couldn't be bothered to think about them.

We finished watching the cartoons together and then Jason came in.

"Who wants a Coke?"

"I do," Clive answered.

"Tanya?"

I nodded.

"There's only four left. We'll have to ask Mum to get some more."

He came back with the Cokes and straws for me and Clive. We all drank them in silence, watching *Junior Kickstart*.

Later, Clive dashed out after hearing something and informed us that the removal van had arrived back with Mum and Gerry. He sounded excited. It was an infectious kind of excitement. Half of me wanted to dash out with him and Jason, to join in the unpacking. But I didn't do anything. I just sat there.

It was chaos. I could hear the chaos. Excitement. Why couldn't I go out and join in? Why did I just

have to sit there, in my shell? Even Tiger had gone
out to investigate. Once again I felt alone. Terribly
alone. I grabbed my notebook. Just doodled until
some words came.

A MOUSE,
IN A HOUSE,
A HOLE,
WITH JUST HIS SOUL.
ALONE. ALONE. ALONE.
CRYING TO BE ALONE.
TRYING TO REMEMBER,
TRYING TO SEE,
WHAT HE COULD BE DOING THERE,
WHO HAD THE KEY.

I read my poem. Of course they didn't care, that was
the trouble. No one wanted to see. No one had the
key. Poor little mouse. He might even be eaten by the
cat. Eaten. Demolished.

Chapter Six

"Hello, Tanya." The doctor sat behind his desk. He was quite an old man, with a craggy face and silvery-grey hair. He smiled. "Well, it's nice to meet you. You're going to have to tell me a bit about yourself. I've got all your notes here but I like to make a few of my own. So are you going to get your notepad ready?"

I did so.

"How old are you now?"

SIXTEEN.

"When's your birthday?"

10TH APRIL.

"So you're coming on seventeen. How long haven't you been talking?"

TWO YEARS.

"That's a long time, isn't it?"

I nodded.

"You've left school now?"

I nodded.

"Your Mum's married and you're living in Cher-ryhurst?"

YES.

"How do you like your new house and family?"

I couldn't answer.

"I see your step-father's a vet."

I still didn't answer.

"Not too pleased, eh?"

I shrugged.

"Why not?"

Silence.

"He's not a cruel step-father, is he?"

Silence.

"Let's go back a bit, shall we? Two years ago. D'you remember when you stopped talking?"

I nodded. Warily, though. Wary of what he was going to say next.

"Tell me the circumstances leading up to that, then."

He made it seem so simple and easy. As if I could tell him just like that. It annoyed me. This stranger whom I'd never met before. This damn doctor. This damn psychiatrist.

For a long time we sat in silence. I was aware of his eyes studying me. Finally he coughed.

"So, you don't want to try."

I did nothing.

"Is it good not talking? D'you get more attention? Well, obviously you do. You've got a problem, haven't you? Most people care if someone's got a problem."

I looked down at my hands.

"I don't believe in pussyfooting around, Tanya. I'm going to be straight with you. I don't think you've got as big a problem as everyone thinks you have. I think you're playing on it. So much so that it could stop you from talking."

His words grated inside me. Every one of them. I felt sick. I wanted to walk out. But I didn't.

"If you don't tell me, Tanya, I'll tell you."

I didn't care. He could do what he wanted. It wouldn't bother me. I'd mentally switched off. He could say anything.

"OK. Your real father. He was cruel. Wasn't he? An alcoholic. Cruel, especially to you. So much so that he had incest with you."

I shook my head.

"It'll do you no good to run from the truth, Tanya. I know it was nasty and once you can talk we'll talk about it. But that wasn't the main problem anyway. You had a baby sister, didn't you?"

I shook my head.

"One day while you and your sister were alone in the house your father came home drunk. You went upstairs and on the landing found your father molesting your sister. You tried to intervene and your father pushed your sister down the stairs. She died. Your father admitted it and was jailed. Now, what I want to know is when you stopped talking and why?"

They didn't know, you see. No one knew. The truth. The truth. Ringing in my ears. Attacking me. Vibrating. They didn't know. They were all imbeciles.

"You see, Tanya, sometimes when people don't talk it's because they're hiding something. But as far as I can see you've got nothing to hide. That's unless, of course, we've got it all wrong."

I smiled. I don't know why. Of course they hadn't got it all wrong. How absurd for the doctor to suggest such a thing. No one had suggested it to me before.

"What's funny? Am I right? Have we got it all wrong?"

I shook my head.

"No?"

I shook my head again.

"You see, the shock of what happened could have

24

well made you not talk, but after two years and with the intensive therapy you've had you should be talking by now, and that's what worries me."

Perhaps I'll never be able to talk again. Never. Ever. Ever.

"You like writing, don't you?"

I nodded.

"Stories? Poems?"

BOTH.

"Will you write me something for next week?"

No one had asked me to do that before. But I didn't mind.

YES.

"Write me a story about the father you wish you'd had."

I looked at him. Wondering if he was serious.

"Write it down so you'll remember. As long as you like. It doesn't matter."

I wrote it down.

"Right then. I'll see you next Friday. The same time."

I rose to leave.

"Goodbye, Tanya."

Mum was in the waiting room. While I had been in with the doctor she'd been talking to his social worker. That was the done thing, apparently, with a new patient.

"Hello, love. All right?"

I nodded.

"Come on then."

I was thinking deeply on the way home. I was thinking about the story I had to write. I was quite pleased in a way. I liked writing things about my

25

feelings. It made me feel happy. It released something within.

I told Mum on my notepad when we arrived home and she seemed quite pleased as well.

"You'll have to tell Sarah. She'll be interested."

I thought perhaps I would. I hadn't had much to do with Sarah. Only sat next to her at meal-times. She was quite busy. In the evening she either went to a Youth Club or was sitting somewhere writing by herself. She told me once that she wanted to be a famous author. She seemed very determined, although she said her writing was a bone of contention between her and her dad; he said it was a selfish career because you did it on your own. In a way her saying that about her father made me feel better about her. She didn't seem quite so bad after that.

At lunchtime, Mum, Gerry and I had fish and chips from the shop. I sat at the kitchen table eating mine and for the first time didn't feel quite so nervous with Gerry sitting opposite me. He had a later surgery that day, that's why we were having lunch at twelve. Mum told him about the story I had to write.

"Homework, eh?" He smiled at me. "What else did he have to say?"

That it was all a con, I thought. A con, on my part. That's what he had to say. Lies. I smiled at Gerry. Lies again. I was twisted. Completely twisted. The funny thing was that I knew it. But I still wasn't going to talk. Lies or no lies.

"Well, did you like him?" Gerry asked.

I shrugged.

"Not sure? When have you got to go again?"

I held up seven fingers.

"Next week?"

I nodded.

"You'll have to get on and write that story then, won't you?"

Chapter Seven

I lay on my bed that afternoon. I usually had a rest in the afternoons, but I couldn't sleep just then. I was thinking about the father I would have liked to have. I remembered I used to dream about it. Oh, many years ago. Before it all happened. When Dad was nothing more than a cruel alcoholic. Sometimes after he'd beaten up Mum I used to lie in bed at night dreaming of a real, good father. He'd be good-looking. He'd have dark hair, not fair like Dad's. We'd play together. Daft games. We'd say stupid things to each other and laugh together about them afterwards. He'd poke me in the stomach. He'd tickle me. He'd kiss me on the forehead. He'd sit on my bed at night and we'd talk together. Oh yes. How my dreams used to flow. I even used to pretend a male teacher at school was my father. He was fat and had a soft voice. A very gentle man. I loved him and some-times I used to pray to a God I didn't believe in to make him my real father. But it never happened. And because it never happened I would cry myself to sleep some nights.

I'm older now, though. Much has happened. I've changed. How would I like a father to be now, I wondered. I took my notepad and pen and sat on the window-sill. I thought for about half an hour before I started to write.

HE WOULD CARE. FIRST AND FORE-
MOST. HE WOULD ALWAYS BE THERE.
HE WOULDN'T CARE IF I DID SOME-
THING WRONG. I MEAN I WOULDN'T
FEEL GUILTY ABOUT IT. SHORT. DARK.
GOOD-LOOKING. HE WOULDN'T DRINK.
HE WOULDN'T SMOKE. I WISH I HAD A
FATHER WHO WOULD LOVE ME FOR
NOTHING. NOTHING IN RETURN. HE
WOULD LOVE MY MUM. HE WOULDN'T
HURT HER. HE WOULDN'T TOUCH US IF
WE DIDN'T WANT TO BE TOUCHED. HE
WOULD ALWAYS TELL THE TRUTH.
ALWAYS GIVE THE RIGHT ADVICE.

I stopped. It was all right, you know. All right
writing all this but what was the point? I suddenly
wondered. There was something going on in my
stomach. Making it gurgle. Something going on
inside my head which I couldn't fathom out. Suddenly I felt angry. I reread what I'd written. I s'pose it
was true, all of it. But I didn't want to know any
more. All about this father business. I didn't want to
know. Gerry. I thought of Gerry. Then my new doctor. Maybe it was a plan. Hatched up by both of
them. I suddenly realized what was bugging me. All
those things I'd written. All those things. Well, perhaps Gerry was all those things. He didn't drink. He
didn't smoke. Etc. Etc. I couldn't bear thinking about
the rest. It was just a plan, to get me to love him. To
get me to want him. To get me to trust him. Yes, even
that. Trust. I picked up my pen again.

I WOULD NEVER WANT TO TRUST A
FATHER AGAIN. BECAUSE ALL MEN ARE

THE SAME. BULLIES. THEY ONLY WANT
ONE THING. I'M TIRED OF MEN. I'M
TIRED OF WRITING. I'M TIRED OF THINK-
ING. I JUST WANT TO SLEEP.

I lay on my bed but sleep wouldn't come. There was a
knot in my heart which made me toss and turn. A
bug. Constantly at me. I couldn't rest. I wasn't at
peace. I kept thinking of Gerry. The more I thought of
him the more I tossed and turned. He was a wasp in
my room. He was an ant in my sock. I had to move. I
couldn't stay on my bed any longer.

I went out the front door because I didn't want to
go through the kitchen. I opened the wooden gate
and closed it again. When I was closing it I happened
to glance up. Gerry's office was at the front of the
house. His desk facing the window. He was at his
desk. Looking straight at me. For a moment I just
stood staring hard at him and he stared back. Then I
moved away from the gate, strode down the road.

I didn't know where I was going except that it was
away from the village. I had no idea the church was
near us but suddenly I saw it. A large brick church,
on the other side of the road. I don't know why I
crossed. I had no intention of going inside the
church. But suddenly I found myself opening the
wooden door.

The peace hit me. It was so peaceful it was like a
noise in my ears. I walked down the main aisle.
Passing the choir stalls. There were wooden chairs on
either side of me. I looked up at a cruxifix on the
church wall. It meant nothing to me. The altar was up
a few steps. With a large, plain cross on it. There was
a candle burning to my left.

I sat back on a seat. Just taking in the peace. I'd never felt that comfortable in a church before. It was welcoming, somehow. Welcomed me. Me? Of all people. What was I? Who was I to be sitting in here? Mum and Gerry, yes. They were true Christians. But me? Here. A church. A holy place. Me? Me? Me?

I didn't believe in God. It was all a fable as far as I was concerned. I never really thought about a God. I couldn't even imagine one. Only someone nasty to heap bad things upon a person. That was my God. A bad God. Not a caring one. But here was I, sitting in church and not feeling bugged any more. There was something which made me feel at ease, which made me feel restful. But why, I wondered. I thought about God. And who else? What about his Son, Jesus Christ. I thought about him. Of course I only knew the things I'd learnt at school and they were a haze in my memory. Jesus.

I looked at the wooden structure on the wall. Jesus. Crucified. On the cross. Wood for wood. Blood for blood. An eye for an eye. Life for life. Was it like that? Here in church? Or was it different from the world? In here. In the peace. Was there a different life? Freedom. To be free. Not caged like a pet mouse. Freedom. That word kept springing to my mind as I looked around the church. It was something. I felt that. There was something. Deep in my soul I felt a yearning. Somewhere. Like a baby's hand clutching out at something. Trying to grasp. Grasp. Grasp. Grasp. Grasping its meaning.

What was it about? I wanted to ask someone. What did it all mean? God. Jesus. Good. Did it mean all good? No wrong. Thou shalt not commit murder.

I shuddered. Felt cold.

Then condemn me, I thought. Now, you God of this world. God of this church. Condemn me now. Kill me. I want to be killed. Send me to hell. Watching eyes. Watching white eyes who have done no wrong. Commit me. Hate me. Loathe me. Do what I want. Do what I deserve. Don't give me love. Don't give me a loving father. Don't. Don't. Don't.

The door opened. I turned around. Sarah was standing there. She came in and shut the door. It wasn't until she walked down towards me that I saw she was crying. I couldn't speak. For the first time in ages I actually wanted to speak. But I couldn't. She sat next to me. Her tears came freely. She was sobbing into a handkerchief. I felt for her. A strange kind of feeling which I'd never experienced before. But I didn't do anything. I just sat there and waited. For about five minutes. Ten minutes it could have been before she stopped crying. Then she blew her nose.

"Sorry," she said. "What a showing. I didn't know you were in here."

I looked at her. Tried to convey something which I felt.

"Oh, it's nothing really. I've just got another rejection, that's all. After four months. I thought that one would get published."

I understood. At once. Her writing. Her books. But I hadn't realized that she'd actually finished one.

"Oh well, try again, I s'pose. If that's what God wants. Though, sometimes the dream he gives me vanishes."

There was silence when she stopped talking. Somehow, though, I knew she wanted to say more.

"It's so difficult, you see. I can't talk to anyone

about it. No one has any faith in me. No one believes I can do it. Dad thinks it's selfish. That it can't come from God. But where the hell else does it come from if it doesn't come from God? I didn't create it. A gift. That's what it is. Although sometimes it seems more like a burden. Gifts come from God. And yet Dad can't even understand that. What does he think I'm capable of? Nothing. He thinks I'm just a nothing. He thinks you should be just a nothing. But it's all right for him to say that because he's something. He's a vet. He's doing something worthwhile."

I listened and felt kind of useful. As if I was the only person on the whole earth whom she could talk to. I listened. And felt it was a gift for me then not to be able to talk.

"I do it for God, and yet Dad thinks I'm being selfish. Art is emotional. Oh no, you can't be emotional. That's it with Dad, he hates emotion. He wouldn't understand my books because they're about people with emotions. And everything has to be straight with him. Even his loving has to be in a set pattern. But I'm not like that. I take after Mum. Dear dear Mum. How I miss her. How I miss her." Then she began crying again. "No one knows how much I miss her," she sobbed. "No one. She understood me. She knew me. God, why did she have to die? Why? If only I could talk to her. Just once more. Just once. For an hour or something. I didn't tell her half the things I could have done, Tanya. I thought she was going to be there, you see? I thought she was immortal. But she wasn't." She sniffed. "She wasn't immortal. But I can still live for her. I have to pretend that she would believe in me. Or I wouldn't go on writing."

I'd never thought, you know. About Clive and

Sarah losing their mother. It just had never occurred to me. I didn't think that they had any problems. Not like me, anyway. But a problem to make anyone cry is a problem. No matter if they can talk or not. I was suddenly enlightened. And oddly enough I felt better because of being so.

"Listen." She wiped her eyes. "I'm sorry to bring this all out to you. I usually come in here to be alone. Just to think things through, away from the house. I honestly didn't mean to burden you, Tanya. You've got enough problems of your own to deal with, let alone mine as well."

I had to do something. Just to say it didn't matter. Just to say her problems mattered as much as mine did. I grabbed her hand, without really thinking. I don't know why, but I started to cry.

"Oh, Tanya." She put her hand over my face. "I'm really glad you've come to live with us. I hoped we would be friends. I know you've got a lot to sort out but I'll help you. We can be friends, can't we?"

I nodded.

"We'll get along all right. It's nice to have someone else to talk to. Thanks, Tanya. I meant that. It's meant a lot to me, you being here."

I couldn't do anything else but cry. She hugged me then and we clung together. I knew I'd made a friend. And I felt so happy. I hadn't had a friend for years. I just hadn't let anyone in.

"Are you coming home for tea?" She wiped my face with her fingers.

I nodded.

"Come on then. Let's go back to the den."

We walked back to the house together. I felt taller somehow. Much taller.

Chapter Eight

At that time in church a bond was made between Sarah and me. A strong bond. I was on her side and I felt that she was on mine. We didn't tell anyone what had happened in church but we were together quite a lot in the house, so they must have known something had.

On Saturday Sarah gave me her book to read. The manuscript was typed neatly and I took it to my bedroom, closed the door and began reading. There was a break for lunch in the middle and then I continued again until I'd finished it. I don't know what I'd been expecting really. I had no thoughts beforehand whether I thought it would be good or not. But if I'd thought it wouldn't be good I'd have been pleasantly surprised. It was good. It held me right the way through. It was about a middle-class girl falling in love with a boy who had just come out of a Youth Custody Centre. Of course the girl's parents were against the relationship, so after a lot of thought she decided to leave home. The book was all about her feelings as she left home and how the boy helped her. The boy, however, began to get into crime again. The girl tried to stop him, but he ended up being sent back to the Centre. She was devastated and returned home after realizing her parents had perhaps been right. Her loving family didn't comdemn her and were really glad to have her back home, and that was the end of the book.

I neatly put the loose papers in order again and put them back in her folder. I took my notepad and pen and began writing.

I THOUGHT IT WAS A LOVELY BOOK. WHY DON'T YOU TRY SENDING IT TO ANOTHER PUBLISHER? YOU'VE GOT AMAZING TALENT. I HAVE EVERY BELIEF IN YOU.
TANYA.

I slipped the note in the folder and took it along to her room. I placed it on her bed and left. As I was returning to my room, I bumped into Mum on the landing.

"Oh, Tanya, here you are. You coming to Maidstone with us? I could buy you some jeans while we're there. Jason and Clive are coming."

I suppose I just felt like going out. I wouldn't have gone normally. But I felt sort of extra confident all of a sudden. Ready to take on the world, so it seemed. Or, anyway, ready to take on my fear of Gerry. I nodded to Mum and she was pleased.

"Get yourself ready then. We're going in about ten minutes."

I sat in the back of Gerry's truck, in between Jason and Clive. It was one of those flash trucks. Large wheels. It seemed as if we were really high up inside. As if we were kings of the road.

"You need a new pair of slippers, don't you, Tanya?" Gerry said, whilst driving.

I caught his eyes in the mirror.

"I'll do you a deal. You say one word from here to Maidstone and I'll buy you a pair." He was serious. As if it was as simple as that to say one word. What the hell did he think anyway? That I'd speak for him?

For a pair of slippers? Oh no. No way.

"Hey, Dad. If I say one word will you buy me a new jumper?"

Gerry laughed at Clive along with Mum.

"I need one for the disco next week. The one I want is in Walkers."

"Who said you were going to the disco next week?"

"Don't be rotten, Dad."

"I haven't made up my mind yet. What d'you think, Jason? Should we let him out on the tiles for the night?"

"If he does all the washing and wiping up for the next few days."

Clive leant over me to thump Jason.

"And Dad, you still haven't answered me about a party for my birthday."

"One thing at a time, Clive. Give me a chance."

"I asked you a week ago."

"He's a very busy man," Mum said.

"Don't I know it. Will you convince him, Kath? That it'll be OK for us to have a party?"

"Oh, do I have to take him out for the night?"

"I'll be staying in if they have a party. Making sure the house isn't ruined."

"Spoilsport," Clive grunted. And nothing more was said on the subject.

We parked in a multi-storey carpark.

"Where are we meeting you, Dad?" Clive said and immediately received a stare from Jason. I saw it and was aware he'd said the wrong thing. But why? I didn't know.

"Tanya," Mum said, "Gerry wants a word with you. We three are going to C & A's. We'll meet you there. Come on, you two. Out you get."

I was trapped, wasn't I? What could I do? Make a run for it? In a strange place I didn't know? I couldn't stalk upstairs to my bedroom. So I just tried to sink further into the car seat and watched the others walk away.

"Are you coming to sit in the front?" Gerry asked.

I said and did nothing. My heart beginning to beat faster. My hackles up. Waiting for him to pounce. Or that's what it seemed like. To me. To my fear.

"All right. I'll come in the back."

I tried to make myself smaller as he sat next to me. I desperately didn't want to touch him. No. No. No.

"I thought I'd take this chance to have a talk to you, Tanya. Without you running off somewhere. You don't have to be frightened. I'm not going to eat you. Or hit you."

Try molesting me, I thought.

"Your mum and I had a word with your doctor yesterday. I went with her because now that we're married you're not only her responsibility, you're mine as well."

Great, I thought. What next? Hatching plans with the doctor. I might have known. I wasn't scared of him, though. Not any more. My heart slowed down. The prickling at the back of my neck ceased .

"You're quite an important girl. We were in there about an hour talking about you."

Fame at last.

"He's a very good doctor, Tanya. He's the top dog around these parts."

Woof, Woof.

"Now, Tanya. I'm going to talk to you straight. We're not going to carry on as we have been. It's going to stop. Avoiding me. Staying in your bedroom. Stalk-ing out when something happens which you don't like. Writing hateful things on paper. You see, Tanya, it's just all becoming a big habit and I don't want you to think you can carry on acting like that in our household. The others can't get away with it. So why should you?"

I buckled inside. Suddenly felt two foot tall. I looked down at my hands. But I'm ill, I wanted to say, I'm ill.

"Just because you can't talk it doesn't mean to say you're ill. In fact the doctor says you're very much better. You're only on the minimum of drugs now and in nine or ten months you could be off them altogether."

God. God God. What's he trying to say? I cringed inside. He was making me feel like an impostor. And I couldn't do anything about it. I just had to sit there and take it.

"You see, it's been very difficult for your mother to cope on her own with you, which hasn't been your fault. But it's meant she's been soft with you when perhaps she could have been harder. We know you've had a bad time. But you're not the only girl to have had an unhappy childhood. You're not the only one in this whole world to have suffered."

I started taking my rings off. I always wore five. I took them off. Dropped them on the floor. Stamped on them. Tried to grind them into the carpet. Wishing that I could grind him into the carpet. Squash him flat.

"You see, things like that won't work with me, Tanya. Not tantrums. Because tantrums are only caused through being spoilt. And I don't like them. So you're just slamming your head against a brick wall as far as I'm concerned."

After dispensing with all my rings I began pulling at

strands of my hair. I didn't care how much I hurt myself, I just had to pull and pull.

"Another thing, your mother has let it go that you can't talk. Whenever she's mentioned the subject of trying to get you to talk you've thrown a tantrum which has made her give up. But I'm not easily put off. You and I are going to have a ten-minute session every day. When you're going to try. Try your hardest to talk."

Pull. Pull. Pull. Chunks of hair now. Chunks of hair.

"I'm not going to give up, Tanya. I'm a very patient man. But neither are you. You're going to try. For the first time you're going to try."

Then what will happen? Then what will happen? What the hell does he think he knows? The truth? Really? Is he running after me? Is he a policeman? Is he that great dark shadow? Open the door in the desert and he's there.

I squeezed my nails into my face.

"I'll tell you what's going to happen. You're going to start being civil around the house. To everyone, not only the cat. You're not going to be rude any more. And another thing. I'll give it a few more weeks. But after that you're going to start looking for a job."

My face hurt where I was slowly bringing my nails down it, drawing blood. He just didn't care, though. He didn't care. The bastard. I hated him. But I couldn't tell him. I just couldn't tell him.

"We'll both help you look for work. Especially if you still can't talk. But you're going to have to start living, Tanya. Get out into the world. Into life. You can't stick around the house for ever doing just as you please."

No. Just as I please. No. Just as I please. No. Just as I please. How come he knew so much anyway? Perhaps it was his God. Up in heaven. His Jesus. Perhaps he will be crucified one day. Then I'll hammer in the nails. Damn him. Damn them all. Damn them all.

"So," he said, "it won't help you tearing your face apart. Because we're going to make a fresh start. From now. Aren't we?"

I pulled my hands away from my face. Felt the blood trickle down. The soreness, which was in my heart and soul as well.

"Aren't we, Tanya?"

I wanted to scream at him. Scream. No. No. No. But I didn't scream. I nodded. Of all the stupidest things to do, I nodded.

"Good. Come on, then, we'd better go and find the others."

We found the others waiting outside C & A's. Mum looked guilty as soon as she saw me. Jason didn't look at me. And Clive just walked on. It was as if everyone knew what had happened. It was that kind of atmosphere. Everyone left me alone, though, and I was grateful for that because just at that moment I didn't feel like starting again and I couldn't have done. Perhaps everyone sensed that and perhaps they even cared.

We went into a number of shops and I tagged on behind. Clive had his jumper and Jason and I had a new pair of jeans each. His was a late birthday present from Mum. I had five pounds of my own money and wanted to spend it, but didn't really know what on. I love the W. H. Smith's shop, though, and Gerry wanted to go in there, so we all traipsed in. We agreed to go our own separate ways and meet outside the shop, so Jason and I went off together.

"You all right, kid?" he asked.

I nodded.

"Good." He ruffled my hair. "What d'you want?"

I was looking at all the stationery. I love things like that. I saw a pack of three-ring notepads and decided to buy them. Then I saw a ring binder with Winnie the Pooh on the front. I don't know why I wanted it really, but I bought that with some paper to go in it.

It cheered me up a bit buying that, and then I followed Jason to the record department because he wanted to buy an LP. He was absolutely ages looking through but finally picked one which was made up of lots of well-known singles.

They were waiting for us when we got outside.

"What d'you get, Jason?" Clive asked.

"A record."

"Let's see."

"When we get home."

"What did you buy, Tanya?" Gerry asked.

I took the file out of the bag and showed him.

"Winnie the Pooh, eh? Very nice. Put it in the bag then."

I put it in Mum's shopping bag. Then she put her arm around me.

"Come on, Tanya. Let's get back to the truck. We'll get home and put some cream on your face."

Chapter Nine

It wasn't bad, you know. Going back home. In the truck I was dreading it. Wondering what I'd do. I thought Gerry would be watching my every move. I thought I wouldn't be allowed to go upstairs to my bedroom. Wouldn't be allowed to do this. Wouldn't be allowed to do that. Anyway, I got in and went straight up to my bedroom. I lay on my bed and pondered. What had he meant? God, he had one over on me, anyway. One over on me. I lay there. Thinking. I s'pose I knew although I could have pretended I didn't. I s'pose I knew really. What he'd meant. Rudeness. I blushed at the realization of it. I'd just ignored him, that was it. Rudeness? Well, yes, perhaps. He could have put it like that. Tantrums? Spoilt? Was I? Really? But he didn't know. He didn't know it all and that's what was so unfair. No one knew it all. Why, though? Why? Why? Why? The word switched on and off in my mind. Because. Because. I can't talk, that's why. It's not an illness, though. Not an illness. So, what does it all boil down to? What? Me? Me? Is it really me? If I could talk I'd tell them. So why can't I talk? Because I'm scared of what might happen if I tell them. That's why. And if that isn't a good enough reason, then what is. I'm scared. I'll be locked up. I'll be sent away. They'll all hate me for what happened.

There was a knock on my door. Then Sarah popped her head round. "Can I come in?"

43

I beckoned to her.

"How did Maidstone go?"

I reached for my notepad and pen. YOUR DAD TALKED TO ME.

"Yeah. I know." She sat on my bed. "Got the works, did you?"

SORT OF.

I shrugged.

"Sorry."

I HAVE TO FIND A JOB SOON.

"Is that what he said?"

YEAH.

"I'm going to give up work soon. Well, I'm only going to work part-time."

WHAT? I was surprised.

"I want to concentrate more on writing. My vow. My secret." She tapped her nose and smiled.

DOES HE KNOW?

"Of course not. He'll go bonkers. He'll get over it, though. He usually does. I've got plenty of money in the bank to pay my keep for a while. My Gran left Clive and me one thousand pounds each in her will."

I THINK YOU'RE BRAVE.

"To go against him? If you want to be famous you have to take risks. Haven't you heard that before?"

I shook my head.

"Well, it's true. I'm not scared of taking risks. So, don't worry, in a few days the heat's going to be off you and on me, so you'll be able to relax a bit."

THANKS. BUT RATHER YOU THAN ME.

"Forget it, Tanya, no hassle. You'll see. What d'you do to your face?"

SCRATCHED IT.

"Did Dad make you?"

44

I nodded.

"You're crazy. Self-destruction. You should love yourself more. Be vain. Like Dad's vain. He's a vain pig at times."

I studied her bright blue eyes.

"Anyway, what I really came to ask you was, would you like to come to the Youth Club with me on Monday night. It'll be no hassle. Everyone's great there. Especially Robin, the leader."

I wasn't sure. My first reaction was to say no straight away. A braver part of me seemed to intervene, though. So, I pondered.

"They won't make fun of you because you can't talk. I've told them about you. My friends would like to meet you. We could cycle. You can borrow Clive's bike or I'll have Clive's and you can have mine. Oh please come, Tanya. I'd love you to."

Why not? The thought suddenly struck me. Take risks if you want to be famous. Well, who said I didn't want to be famous?

OK, I wrote, OK.

"Great stuff, Tans. It'll do you good. Get out of this place. I'll be looking forward to it." She practically bounced off my bed.

"Tea's nearly ready, I think. You coming down?"

I nodded. Suddenly much happier.

Chapter Ten

The whole lot of us watched a film on telly that night. It was the first time I'd actually sat with them all in the lounge. It was a murder mystery and a bit spooky, so I got into the film and soon forgot about the surroundings. Well, forgot about me being in the same room as Gerry.

The film finished at nine and we all stretched and yawned.

"What's on now?" Clive asked.

"News," Gerry said.

"Yuk. Can't we turn over?"

"Your step-mother wants to watch the News."

"Who wants to play Monopoly? Sarah?"

"You can't play that at this time of night."

"Well, why don't you play something else?" Mum suggested, which I could have throttled her for. I was hoping I could retire to my bedroom then. So I didn't have to stay any longer with Gerry.

"What about Ludo?" she said. "All four of you could play. And you, Jason. All four of you."

"Yeah, OK. What about it? Will you play, Jason?"

"As long as I can be red I'll play."

"Spot the baby." Clive bounced out of the room.

"I s'pose we've been roped in, Tanya," Sarah said.

"Get the small table out, Tanya. It's in the dining room. You can play on that."

I did as Gerry said and brought it into the lounge,

out of the way of the telly. I s'pose I didn't feel too bad about playing then. I had a sort of excited feeling.

"You can be referee, Dad," Clive said as he came in with the Ludo.

"Don't be daft. We don't need a referee." Jason grabbed the box and set the game on the table.

"We do if you play because you probably cheat."

"Ha, ha."

"What colour am I?" Sarah asked. "Yellow? Sit here, Tanya, and you can be green."

"That means I don't have a choice," Clive grumbled.

"Isn't that a shame?"

"I'll sit on the pouffe."

"You do that."

"Go on. Throw the dice, Jason, and I hope you get a one."

Jason happened to get a five and it was the highest score, so he went first.

I enjoyed it. For the first time in ages I actually enjoyed doing something with other people. We had fun. Laughing. Joking. Especially when we kept taking each other's counters.

Jason won. Sarah came second, and then it was between me and Clive. I was glad he beat me. I didn't think he'd like completely losing. And I didn't mind losing. It had just been a good game. I felt exhilarated afterwards. I even managed a smile at Gerry.

"Right. Drinks and then bed," Gerry said.

"Go and take your tablets, Tanya," Mum said. "I'll come and make the drinks."

We had our night-time drinks together in the lounge. I

felt tired. I usually went to bed at about nine-thirty, but now it was nearly eleven.

"Well, big day tomorrow at church," Gerry said. "Is everyone looking forward to it?"

I must admit I'd forgotten. The vicar of the church Mum and Gerry go to was retiring shortly and was having a meal for all the church people to celebrate. All the congregation. The vicar and his wife didn't have any children and Mum once told me that Gerry was like a son to them. They'd been really close for years. That was why all of our family were going to be sitting on the head table with the vicar. So we'd all be on show, so to speak. I s'pose I wasn't really looking forward to it. I was nervy. But I felt better about it than I had about Mum's and Gerry's wedding. So perhaps it wouldn't be that bad.

"We don't have to go to church first, do we?" Clive asked.

"No."

"I'm going," Mum said. "Tanya, are you coming with me?"

"I'll come with you," Sarah said.

"Tanya?"

I really wasn't sure. I hadn't been to a normal church service for years. Not since I'd been confirmed, when I was ten.

"Well, see if you wake up on time," Gerry said. "If not, you could come to the six-thirty service. Not so many people go to that. You won't feel so overpowered."

"She doesn't believe in God anyway," Clive said. "Like me."

"You just keep out of it and get to bed."

"All right, Dad." He kissed Mum goodnight and a

pang of jealousy jumped in my stomach. For a minute I hated him.

"Don't spend ages in the bathroom," Jason said.

"Dad, tell him to stop picking on me."

"Just because I won," Jason smiled.

"Jason, stop getting at him."

"Mother!"

"Well, you are."

"Ho. Ho. Ho." Clive leapt out of the room. With Jason going after him.

"All right, Sarah?" Gerry asked.

"Yeah. I don't know what to wear tomorrow."

"Wear the dress you wore to the wedding," Mum suggested.

"Yeah, I could do, as long as it doesn't smell."

"Well, you've only worn it once, darling."

"I could wear my trouser suit. Would that be the done thing? Not that I care if it isn't. But I can hardly turn up in jeans."

"You could do anything," Gerry said. "You've got some front, haven't you?"

"Very funny. Oh, I'll see tomorrow. I'm going to bed. You coming up, Dad?"

"I'll be up,"

"See yer then. Night, Kathy." She kissed her on the cheek.

"Night, love. God bless."

"Coming, Tanya?"

I nodded.

"We'll be up, Tanya," Gerry said, as we went through the door.

We'll be up, Tanya. I had the jitters as I was lying in bed thinking of that. Mum usually came into my

49

room at night but never Gerry. But then I thought of the evening. The first night I'd ever stayed down with them and it had gone all right. I'd enjoyed it. So perhaps it would be all right after all. Everything. Perhaps Gerry wasn't so bad. Perhaps it had been a good thing that Mum and Gerry had got married. Oh, I didn't know. Suddenly so much had changed. It wasn't just Mum, Jason and I any more. I couldn't do as I pleased any more. I couldn't shut everything off like I had been doing. Why not? Why couldn't I just carry on like before? Why? Because of him. A man. A man. A monster? A monster because of the secret he knew. A secret I didn't dare talk about. What about tomorrow? On parade in front of all those good people. Christians? Is that who they were? Christians. So what am I? Who am I?

I heard Mum and Gerry come upstairs. They passed my room and I heard them talking to Clive. He didn't believe in God, he'd said. He didn't believe in God and neither did I. But there were some questions lingering in my mind. Some questions which mattered. Which I needed the answers for. In the darkness I reached for my notepad and pen. Then I switched my bedside light on. I had to do it. Ask Gerry the questions, although fear was bouncing in my heart. I had to do it.

WHAT DID JESUS DIE FOR?
DOES GOD FORGIVE EVERYONE?

I sat in my bed and waited for them to come in.

"You still up, love?" Mum came in first.

I nodded.

Then Gerry came in. They both sat on the side of my bed. I turned my notepad over and wrote to Mum.

I'VE GOT SOMETHING TO ASK GERRY.

"Well, go ahead then. She wants to ask you something, Gerry. Have you written it down?"

I nodded. Passing the questions over. I felt myself blush because of the type of questions they were.

They read them together.

"Well," Gerry said, "they're tough questions for this time of night. But I think I can manage them."

"I think I'll leave you two to it. I'll go and see Sarah," Mum said. "Goodnight, love. God bless." She kissed me on the cheek, I held her hand for a while; tightly. "You'll be all right," she assured me; understanding.

Gerry moved nearer me to where Mum had been sitting. "Well," he said. "What did Jesus die for? Basically, love, he died for us. He died to forgive us for our sins. You see, God gave us his Son so that whoever may believe in him will be saved. Will have eternal life. Will find true peace."

FOR OUR SINS?

"If you repent of your sins, they will be forgiven."

WHAT ARE SINS?

"We all fall short. Only Jesus was perfect. We all sin. In many ways. Every day."

BUT SOME SIN MORE THAN OTHERS. BIG SIN. WHAT ABOUT THOSE PEOPLE? LIKE THE PEOPLE WHO GET SENT TO PRISON.

"It's the same with them. If they believe in the Lord Jesus Christ and repent of all their sins, truly repent, they will be forgiven."

NOT BY PEOPLE, THOUGH.

"Some people won't forgive. Some people don't know how to. The world doesn't know how to forgive. But if you believe in Jesus Christ you're not of the world."

It all seemed too easy. So you can do anything and be forgiven. So you can do it again and again and again and still be forgiven.

"What're you puzzled about?"

SO I COULD DO SOMETHING TIME AND TIME AGAIN AND STILL BE FORGIVEN?

"If you believed in Jesus you'd try not to sin. If you try he'll see that. If you gain strength from him you can try not to sin. You know if you sin, Tanya. You feel it inside. Your conscience tells you. You can't run from yourself. Well, people can try to but they end up nowhere."

I sighed. There was a lot to think about.

"Sometimes, though, the most difficult part, Tanya, is forgiving yourself. You have to learn to forgive yourself. Some people find that very hard to do."

I leapt inside. That, now that struck home.

"You see, it all ties up with both of your questions. God will and does forgive. That's why he sent his only Son. So that we could be saved."

IF YOU BELIEVE IN HIM.

"Well, we've got free choice. It's up to us."

I nodded.

"Have I answered your questions?"

I nodded again.

"Think about it. Try to grasp the full meaning. It might take time. Don't worry. Anyway, I'll be late for my eight o'clock church warden's duties tomorrow if I don't get to bed. You settle down." He took my notepad and pen from me and put them to one side. Then he switched out my light.

"Goodnight then, love. Well done, you're doing fine. I'm pleased with you." He kissed me on the forehead. "See you in the morning."

He'd kissed me on the forehead and I hadn't flin-
ched. That was something. He said he was pleased.
That was something else. God forgives. He really
forgives. I wondered then. I really wondered then if
there was a God. If there was a Jesus. I went to sleep
wondering. And had no nightmares.

Chapter Eleven

The church hall was absolutely packed. Full of round tables and chairs. All sorts of different people crowded in. Someone showed us to the head table. Which was a long one at one end of the hall. Our places were marked and I was sitting next to Mum and Jason.

We all clapped when the vicar, Herbert, and his wife came in, and then everyone stood while Herbert spoke a few words of grace before we all sat again and began to eat.

It was a salad meal with different meats. I was nearly too nervous to eat but after a glass of wine I didn't feel so bad. And I managed to forget how I looked. How I appeared to the public eye. To other people who were seeing me for the first time. When I was brave enough to look up I didn't see anyone staring at me, which I thought they would be. So I felt better.

It took about three quarters of an hour for everyone to finish eating. Then Gerry stood and banged a hammer on the table. There was a sudden hush in the hall. I'd never heard Gerry speak in public before and I wondered how he'd do it, knowing that even if I could talk I wouldn't be able to do such a thing. He was so relaxed, though. So full of confidence. He was talking about Herbert and how much everyone had valued and admired him as a vicar. How much everyone would miss him and that he'd been a great pillar of society. Then he talked about him retiring and how everyone hoped he and his wife would be really happy and enjoy the countryside in Devon. He went on a bit more, talking and joking about this and that, and then he proposed a toast and we all stood again. After that the vicar stood and made a speech. Thanking everyone for the cards and presents. And saying he thought he'd had the best congregation in the country and that he hoped they'd all be happy with the new vicar. Actually he rambled on a bit, until I was getting bored. Finally he sat down, with everyone clapping. Then Sarah stood and walked round to a corner of the hall where she picked up a bouquet of flowers. She brought them round and gave them to Herbert's wife, kissing her. Everyone clapped again and for a strange moment I felt eyes upon me and instead of feeling nervous, I felt important. For once in my life I felt important.

Everyone started rising and walking out to the lobby and the kitchen. Mum and Gerry disappeared into a throng of people. I drank more wine and felt quite merry.

"You coming down?" Jason asked. "I'm going to get some more wine. D'you want some?"

I nodded. Gave him my glass.

"I feel like getting pissed." Jason winked. I thumped him on the arm but felt the same.

As we were making our way through the people everyone seemed to be smiling at us. Jason said hello to everyone and I just smiled back, praying no one would actually talk to me. We went to the kitchen, where a tall man with a moustache greeted my brother.

"Hello, Jason. How are you? Settling in to your new life with Gerry?"

"Yes thanks. This is Tanya."

"Oh, Tanya, hello. Greg, that's me."

I shook his hand. But he didn't seem to expect anything more from me.

"Is there any more wine left?" Jason asked.

"Wine? Yes. White or red."

"White, please."

"Here you are."

"Tanya too."

He filled my glass to the top. I laughed. I suddenly felt funnily wicked. And happy. So damn stupidly happy.

The lobby was packed with people and Jason disappeared, so I was frighteningly left on my own.

I leant up against a wall and drank more wine.

An old man sauntered up to me. He smiled. "Hello," he said.

I just smiled.

"Don't worry. I know you can't talk. Been deserted, have you?"

I nodded.

"You're Gerry's new daughter, aren't you?"

I nodded.

"My wife and I were so pleased to hear of the marriage. It's been hard for Gerry with his work and the children. Coping on his own. It'll do him good having Kathy around."

I could have agreed if I could have spoken. I felt in a wonderfully agreeable kind of mood.

"You still at school, are you?"

I shook my head.

"So you'll be looking for a job?"

"Mm."

"Well, I don't know what you want to do. But my son owns a dry-cleaner's. He's looking for someone to train on a Hoffman press. You know, pressing the clothes. It's in Alderton. Only a couple of miles from here. He's been looking for someone for about two weeks now. Would you be interested?"

I nodded. Just like that. God knows why. But as I said, I felt in an agreeable kind of mood.

"He and his family are here today. I'll find Mike and have a word. You just stay there, love. I know he thinks the world of Gerry. I'll go and see him."

I sat on a table in the lobby and felt excited. Hey, guess what, if I landed a job. If I could go and tell Mum and Gerry I'd got a job. As quickly as that. Would they be pleased but would they be pleased. Tra la la.

While I was waiting Clive came to inform me that he was going home.

"You coming?"

I shook my head.

"Jason told Dad that you're drunk."

I smiled.

"Are you?"

I shrugged.

"Disgusting. Perfectly disgusting. See yer later."

I waved him away. Then the old man came back with another short, slightly fat man wearing glasses.

"Hello." He shook my hand.

"This is my son, Mike. Tanya, you're Tanya, aren't you?"

I nodded.

"He knows your problem," the man whispered in my ear. "So don't worry. I'll leave you to it."

"So?" Mike said. "You're after a job."

I nodded.

"What d'you want to do?"

I shrugged.

"Well. It's as simple as this. I'm prepared to give you a try. Just to see how you get on. Some people take to it and some people don't. I'll give you a month's trial and we'll take it from there." He smiled, a warm genuine smile.

I wanted to say thank you. Instead I shook his hand again.

"Gerry knows where the shop is. When d'you want to start? Or shall I have a word with Gerry first?"

I nodded.

"OK, leave it with me then, and I'll sort something out with him."

I stood. Beaming. So happy.

"And hey," he said, before going, "don't drink too much of that today or you'll have a hangover in the morning."

I could have leapt with excitement. I wanted to find that old man again because he'd made it all happen. I wanted to shake him by the hand. I went into the main hall and found him helping to clear the tables.

"You've got the job." I guess he could tell by my face.

I nodded.

"Congratulations. That's wonderful. They're a good bunch of youngsters in that shop. You'll get on well with them. I do a spot of cleaning there in the mornings, so I'll probably see you there then."

I nodded. Took him by the hand. It was the only way I could say thanks. He seemed to understand.

"That's all right, love. I hope you like it."

"Who's he?" Jason came over to me after I'd left the gentleman.

I tapped my nose.

"Hey, what's happened? You're excited about something."

I tapped my nose again and winked at him.

"Tell me when I get home, kid." He pointed a finger at me. "Or there'll be trouble."

I nodded again.

Of course I'd tell him. I felt like telling the whole world. I've got a job. I've got a job. I've got a job. And I'm happy. Happy. Really happy.

I practically skipped back to the house. I walked through the back gate and Tiger was waiting outside the open kitchen door. I picked her up, hugging and kissing her. She purred and dribbled. Followed me in when I went. I put the oven on. Then put the kettle on for a cup of coffee. I went upstairs to change out of my dress, still feeling half tipsy. Tiger followed me into my bedroom and jumped on my bed. I lay there loving her for a while. Until I started to sneeze. Her fur made me do that sometimes.

I changed and skipped downstairs. I just couldn't wait until Mum came home to tell her about the job. I hadn't guessed that she might have been told already.

I grabbed my notepad and wrote. I just had to express myself in some way.

HAPPINESS IS,
HAPPINESS WAS,
ONCE UPON A TIME,
BUT NOW,
AGAIN,

59

THERE IS A GLOW,
FOR ME TO SHOW,
WITHOUT A SHADOW,
A LIGHT SO STRONG,
HAS MADE A NEW SONG,
AND I'M BEGINNING TO WONDER,
IF SOMETHING MORE IS ASUNDER,
IF I TRY,
WILL I GET BY,
PERHAPS IT'LL BE OK,
IF THEY ALL SAY,
AND THERE'LL BE A NEW DAY,
A NEW BREATH,
ON MY LIPS,
TO MAKE WORDS,
TO MAKE WORDS,
PLEASE,
IF IT'S POSSIBLE,
I'LL TRY.

I stopped writing. Felt calmer. More able to contain myself. More able to wait in peace for them to come home.

Chapter Twelve

Of course they both knew. Mum hugged me as soon as she saw me.

"Congratulations, love."

"Well done, Tanya." Gerry ruffled my hair. He actually touched me again. For a dreadful moment I thought it was all going to come back. The darkness. But I caught Gerry's brown eyes. They were hard on me. Just for a few seconds. "You won't be starting until next Monday. It'll give you this week to get a bit more settled in. Is that all right? Next Monday."

I nodded. The darkness hadn't come back. I had to think of the good things.

WHERE'S JASON. I wrote.

"Helping wash up," Mum said.

"It's his excuse to drink more wine," Gerry said. "Right, I must go up and change."

"Yeah, so must I," Mum said.

I was left alone in the kitchen. Me and my coffee. Alone. To think. Again. Everything had gone so well that morning. I couldn't remember when something quite so nerve-racking had gone as well as that. I wondered why. We'd only been here just over a week. And yet I felt so much better. Happier. When a week ago I was hating the thought of living with another man. Yet the week had gone so well. Some of the shadows had gone. Perhaps it was because of him. Gerry. Another man. But a different man. Kind. Loving. Perhaps it had made me feel better when he'd given me his rules. Perhaps it had given me a strong guideline. What I could do or what I couldn't do. He didn't just tell me off for the sake of it. He didn't just lash out because he was drunk. He wasn't like that. And he loved Mum. That was obvious. I'd never lived with a man before who really loved Mum. It was good to see her so happy. And church, I s'pose church had something to do with it. I'm not a born-again Christian, whatever that is supposed to mean. But I think I do believe in God now. I don't know why, really. It just seems more plausible. More so than it has ever seemed before. More believable. He forgives and that's what I was hanging on to. I used to think that no one could ever possibly forgive me. For that. No one knew, but I felt that perhaps God knew. It helped thinking that. Made me feel more at ease with myself. Perhaps God knew and perhaps he would forgive.

Of course I still wasn't talking. Perhaps that would take longer than a week. Perhaps these new tablets the new doctor has put me on will help. Perhaps I've just realized it's all down to me. All down to me. There's no such word as can't. It's either I want or I don't want. Well, do I want now? Do I want when I'd never wanted before? Because there's so much more life here now. So much more excitement. So much more which needs to be said. Sarah. Clive. Not only Jason. Gerry, not only Mum. A new family. Perhaps a family which for a long time had just been in my dreams. In my dreams before it had been cut out by shock. Cut out by my need to withdraw from the world. My dreams. Perhaps the realization of them so suddenly had made me remember the happier times. Before my real father became an alcoholic. Had taken me back to before that shock, so that I could relate now, feel myself a part again. Not exiled. Not in danger of being swallowed by some unearthly monster. Not in danger. Yet I still held that secret.

All I can remember about my real father is shame. Rolling along the streets, drunk. Fighting with other men. All our neighbours looked at him with disgust. They hated him. It was a pleasant surprise to find how much people liked Gerry. It was completely the opposite to Dad. Everyone seemed to respect Gerry. He was an important figure. He wasn't someone to be ashamed of. That meant something to me. Something good. It helped me. Made me feel important because I was a part of that important man. It all added up, you see. This week. Why I found myself accepting more, when before I just ran. It all added up. This week. Why I found myself happier, when before happiness seemed to forever elude me. I had to work it out, you see. In my own mind. Why it had all happened so quickly. Oh, perhaps I'm feeling so happy because of the wine. But apart from that I could still shut Gerry out. I could still withdraw into my shell. I could do. If I wanted. But perhaps, finally, I'd had enough. Perhaps I was tired of it all. Perhaps my new family offered something more than my own small world could offer. Perhaps I could see a light through the darkness. A light. People. Friendship. Perhaps I didn't want to be alone any more. Alone to fight my own battle. Perhaps that. Perhaps. Perhaps. Perhaps.

*

By the time we'd finished tea that day and done all the washing and wiping up it was ten to five. Everyone knew then about my job. Jason, Sarah and Clive. They were all pleased for me. And Sarah told everyone I was going up to the Youth Club with her. Which I'd half forgotten about.

I was sitting in the lounge reading the paper, with Clive sprawled on the floor reading a book, when Gerry came in.

"Tanya. Our ten minutes. Come on. In the office."

That was something else I'd forgotten about in all our excitement. Nerves jingled slightly as I followed Gerry into his office. I'd never actually been in there before. It was quite smart. Full of books. Mum told me he studied in there sometimes. All about different animals' diseases. There was a couch in there and a large chair. I sat on the chair.

"Right." Gerry sat on his swivel desk chair. "Where are we going to start?"

I didn't know. Talk. That's what I was meant to be trying to do. Talk. But how d'you try to talk when you haven't spoken for two years? How do you try? I didn't know.

"I know this is going to be difficult for you. Tanya. We're going to go over things a bit. It may be agony but it's only going to be for ten minutes or so."

Over things? Fear etched a carving in my stomach.

"You'll want to write, so I'll give you my notepad and pen."

It was a fountain pen. My hand sweated around it. Waiting. Just waiting. Dreading.

"Now. Write this date down. July 5th 1984."

64

I wrote July 5th and then stopped. It was too much. I knew the date, you see. I knew the date.

"Written it?"

I just stared down at the paper.

"Try, Tanya. It's only a date."

Only? That was funny. Only? The date. That's what it happened to be. The date.

Sweat trickled down the side of my face. My vision was blurred. I wrote the numbers: 1 9 8 4.

"Now relax, come on. No one's going to jump on you. Tiger's not around at the moment," he smiled. "So, July 5th 1984. You remember?"

I nodded.

"You've written it. Now try to say it."

I looked at him. Into his eyes. I could have got down on my knees and pleaded with him to stop.

"Try, Tanya."

I couldn't. I honestly couldn't. I moved my lips. Tried. Did I try? Could I have talked if I'd wanted to? Did I want to? That date. That date. Stuck in my throat. I shook my head. Flung the notepad on the floor.

"Pick it up."

I shook my head.

"Pick it up."

I wanted to go. Get away from him. He was too powerful. Too close. Too strong. He was too strong. And that suddenly clicked with me. Mentally strong, he was.

"I won't tell you again, Tanya."

I picked the notepad up.

"OK, now write some more. Just one sentence about what happened on that day."

Five minutes passed. Ten minutes passed. Fifteen

minutes passed. Silence. Nothing.

TEN MINUTES HAS GONE. I scrawled on the pad and showed it to him.

"And I want you to do one more thing before we've finished. Just one sentence, Tanya. I'm a patient man."

I began crying. I couldn't see a way out. I couldn't just walk out. I had to stay there. But I couldn't. I just couldn't do what he was asking.

"Listen, Tanya. I'll leave you, OK? I'll leave you in here. So you can take it easy. Take your time. Just anything will do, anything about that day. A few words, that's all I'm asking. A few words, all right? I'll leave you."

I sobbed my heart out, left alone. I looked at the wretched paper in front of me. A few words. A few words.

I blew my nose. Tried to control my shaking limbs. It wasn't quite so bad now that he wasn't watching me. It wasn't quite so bad. I tried to think. Just a few words. About that day. I didn't have to say those words, did I? Not those words. Those which kept plummeting through my mind at about a hundred miles an hour. I didn't have to write down those words. So any would do. Just about that day. That day. I wiped my sweating hands down my jumper. I took hold of the pen. Slowly I wrote. Very slowly.

SALLY WAS THERE. DAD WAS THERE.

When I finished I read my words. But, oh God, how it brought it back. Sally. Sally. How old was she then? Just five. Long blonde hair. Large blue eyes. Oh God. I felt sick. I had to go to the bathroom. I put the pad and pen on his desk and rushed upstairs.

I retched in the loo. Again and again.

"Tanya?" Mum's voice. Mum. I collapsed against her. Crying again.

"Oh, darling, come on. Sit down. Stop it, love. Don't cry so much."

I sat on the bathroom chair and she pressed my head against her breasts. I could hear her heart beat. It calmed me.

"You just sit there. I'll clear this up."

She did as she said. Then she rinsed a flannel and wiped my face.

"What's wrong, Mum?" Jason was at the door.

"It's all right. Tanya's just been a bit sick. Go and make us a cup of tea, love, will you?"

"Yeah, OK."

"All right, Tanya?"

I nodded. The taste of sick bitter in my mouth.

"D'you want your notepad?"

I nodded.

"I'll go and get it."

She came back with it and a pen.

I CAN'T TALK.

"It'll take time, love."

HE THINKS I CAN TALK. I CAN'T. I CAN'T REMEMBER. I DON'T WANT TO REMEMBER. WHY CAN'T WE JUST FORGET IT?

She stroked my hair. "Because you can't talk, love. That's why. Something's stopping you."

I DON'T CARE. PERHAPS I'LL NEVER BE ABLE TO TALK AGAIN.

"But the doctors say there's no medical reason why you can't talk. They say it's you putting a block up. When you can drop that you'll be able to talk."

I DON'T WANT TO TALK.

"Why? Tell me why?"

67

NO ONE UNDERSTANDS.

"We're trying. But only you can truly help us. You're the only one who knows what's going on inside your head."

I DON'T WANT TO GO IN THE OFFICE WITH HIM AGAIN.

She sighed.

DO I HAVE TO?

"He wants you to."

IS HE A HARD MAN?

"Stubborn more than hard."

I THINK HE'S HARD.

"Come on, let's go downstairs and have a cup of tea. Gerry's gone out."

We went downstairs and sat in the kitchen. Jason had made the tea and Mum put three sugars in mine.

Sarah came in and sat with us. We were all sort of glum.

"He's a pighead," Sarah said.

"Sarah!" Mum chided.

"Yeah, shut up, Sarah," Jason said.

"And what do you know? You've only been living here for a week."

"Stop arguing, you two. Come on, let's not spoil this day."

"He already has."

"He's doing his best."

"Well, don't worry, Tanya," Sarah said, going out. "It'll be me tomorrow. I'll spoil his day even more."

"What did she mean by that?" Mum looked at Jason.

He shrugged.

I knew, of course. About her job. But it didn't make me feel any better. He'd got too close, that man called

68

Gerry. Too damn close. And he wasn't going to give up either. He wasn't going to give up. I suddenly felt knackered. All I wanted to do was go to bed.

I WANT TO GO TO BED.

"All right, love. You go up and get ready. I'll be in to see you. I'll bring you your tablets."

Chapter Thirteen

Mum started back to work the next day, so she left early. Before I was awake. Clive had gone to school and Jason to work. I couldn't hear anything downstairs so presumed Gerry was out as well. I stayed in bed reading for a while. Then I got up and dressed. I made myself a cup of coffee and some toast. Gerry wasn't in. I switched the radio on and tuned into Capital Radio. I remembered what had happened the evening before. I wasn't looking forward to seeing Gerry. Then I wondered if Sarah had told him about her job. I wondered what sort of a mood he'd be in. And that worried me. I wished Mum hadn't gone to work. I felt safer with her around.

I finished my breakfast, then started on the washing up, which had been left. I'd just started the wiping when Gerry came in.

"Morning, Tanya. I'm just popping in. On my way to the Blue Cross Clinic. Is there a cup of coffee going?"

I moved to the kettle.

"Good girl. I've just got to make a phone call."

I made his coffee and left it on the table. Then I finished the wiping up. He came in as I was putting everything away.

"We'll have to think about what we're having for dinner tonight. We can get it cooking before Mum gets home. What shall we have? Kath said something

70

about shepherd's pie. Mince. Mince. Mince. Let's have a look." He opened the freezer. "Yeah, here we are. That'll do. D'you want to peel some potatoes and veg. sometime today? And I'll do the rest later."

I nodded.

"I'll get some out, then. We could have some carrots with it. D'you like carrots? They make you see in the dark. There you are. You can do all that lot for me. All right?"

I nodded.

"Right. Coffee. Put sugar in?"

I nodded.

"Good girl, you're learning. By the way, thanks for the words last night."

I looked at him. He winked at me.

I went through to the lounge and began reading. Gerry popped in to tell me he was going but apart from that I wasn't disturbed in my reading all morning.

When I heard the back door open at about quarter past one I thought it was Gerry again so didn't take much notice. But suddenly Sarah popped her head round the door.

"Hiya, Tanya." She was in her dirty working gear.

I was so surprised to see her, I followed her upstairs and grabbed my notepad on the way.

WHAT'RE YOU DOING HOME?

"Hey, part-time, I told you."

ALREADY?

"Yeah. I told them at work ages ago."

DOES GERRY KNOW?

"I didn't have the guts to tell him last night after all."

I was absolutely amazed at her. I sat on her bed and watched her change.

"Is Dad due back?"

71

I shrugged.

"Well, I think there might be fireworks when he does come back. So, if I were you I'd keep out the way."

AREN'T YOU WORRIED?

"Shitting myself, darling. But it has to be done. The sooner, the better."

The sooner, the better. Well, that's what she said. He came in at three when I was peeling the potatoes. Sarah was in the lounge. I felt nervous. For her.

He came in quite happy. But then Sarah suddenly appeared in front of him.

"Sarah? What's wrong? Are you ill?"

"Come in the lounge, Dad. I've got something to tell you."

God. Fireworks. Is that what she said? He went crazy. Talk about yell. Did he yell or didn't he yell. Fireworks. The most expensive ones out, it seemed. And never-ending. But Sarah was no daisy either. She shouted back and I could hear practically every word. She shouted and he yelled and I wondered if they were actually coming to blows in there.

"Just get up to your room. I don't want to see you."

"I don't want to see you much either."

"Don't answer me back."

"You ask for it."

"Get upstairs and stay up there. Until I tell you otherwise."

"I'm going. I'm going. I'll be writing, though, that's what I'll be doing."

"You do that and see where it gets you."

"Fame, Father," she screamed down the stairs. "Fame, that's where it's going to get me."

"A good hiding, that's what it will get you. You're not too old, you know."

Wow! What a cracker! The peace afterwards seemed heaven-sent. I don't know where Gerry went but he didn't come into the kitchen and he didn't go upstairs. I heard a door slam and presumed he'd gone to his office. I whistled to myself. What a one Sarah was, though. She gave as good as she got. I felt sort of proud of her.

I wondered after I'd done all the vegetables whether I should go up and see her, but decided against it. I thought I'd give her time to cool down a bit. So I took my crime thriller up again and settled in the lounge.

Nothing much happened. Clive came home from school. Jason from work. Gerry went out again and Sarah stayed in her bedroom. My peace was shattered, though, because Jason and Clive started a game of cards for money and were arguing no end over it. I didn't bother to tell them what had happened. I thought they'd find out soon enough. Well, they knew Gerry was in a mood when he came in again.

"Turn the telly off," he said, coming into the lounge.

"Oh, Dad."

"Have you got any homework, Clive?"

"Just an essay."

"Go upstairs and do it. Jason, I said turn the telly off and you can lay the table. I didn't mean in an hour's time."

"What's wrong with you?"

"I just want some order in this house. Is that too much to ask?"

"OK, I'll lay the table." He turned the telly off.

"Christ! What's wrong with him?" he asked when Gerry had gone.

I tapped my nose.

"You know everything?"

I nodded.

"You don't want to write an essay for me, do you, Tanya?" Clive asked.

WHAT ABOUT?

"Of all the stupidest things. Anything about an old man."

YOU DO IT.

"I can't think."

YOU WILL.

"Just give me an idea."

I thought a while. ABOUT YOUR GRANDAD DYING.

"Trust you to be morbid."

WELL, IT'S AN IDEA.

"I s'pose I'd better go up. I hope your mother's in a good mood."

Chapter Fourteen

In a funny sort of way I felt sorry for Gerry when I went out to the kitchen and found him preparing the meal. I don't know why. He looked sort of browbeaten. As if he was really worried. Perhaps he really cared.

I decided not to bother him, though. And went upstairs. I knocked on Sarah's door.

"Come in . . . oh hi, Tanya. Sit down."

ARE YOU ALL RIGHT?

"Of course I am. Don't worry. Show's over. The worst has been done, so to speak." She was sitting at her desk, pen in hand.

WHAT YOU DOING?

"New book."

WHAT ABOUT?

"Actually, I don't really know at the moment. I'm just starting. I never plan these things. It just comes."

LUCKY YOU.

"Or not so lucky, as the case may be. I'm dying of thirst. You couldn't sneak me up a Coke, could you?"

I did so. Gerry didn't take much notice of me going to the fridge. I took it up to her.

"Cor, ta. When's your mum due home?"

ABOUT HALF FIVE.

"I'm relying on her, you know."

WHY?

"To be just a bit on my side."

75

I shrugged. I honestly didn't know what she'd think.

"Oh well, Dad's always gorgeous when he's calmed down a bit. It could take a while, though. I don't know if I'll be allowed to go to the Youth Club tonight. But as he knows you're going as well it might be different."

I HOPE SO.

"You could go and say something like, what time will Sarah and I be going to the Youth Club. You know, pepper him up a bit."

I smiled at her. She was funny sometimes.

"Have you had your ten minutes yet?"

NO.

"Do well. And then pepper him up. For me, darling, please."

OK. I'LL TRY.

"Do your bit, babe. Then we can have a good night."

I wandered downstairs and into the kitchen. I took my notepad.

D'YOU WANT ANY HELP?

I showed it to him.

"No. I'm just waiting for the mince to cook."

D'YOU WANT TEN MINUTES YET? I was being braver than I felt.

He looked at me. Surprised. I smiled.

"I'll get the pie put in the oven first, then I'll call you."

He called me about half an hour later. By that time I'd managed to work up quite a sweat. I'd thought of a sentence, though, which I could write. I had it in my mind all ready.

I sat on the rocking-chair, waiting.

"What's Sarah been saying to you? Put on a good show? Get me in a good mood?"

I frowned. Tried to look innocent. But it was as if his eyes could look right through me.

"Want to go to the Youth Club, do you?"

I nodded.

"Perhaps on Wednesday."

I grabbed my notepad. DON'T BE CROSS WITH HER.

"Sometimes she has these things coming."

YOU DON'T UNDERSTAND.

He sighed. "No, probably not. Although I do try. But one can get very tired of trying. You must know that. Besides, she's done a very silly thing. Going part-time. She needs to be out, not stuck at home."

I couldn't think of anything to say to that.

"Anyway, Tanya, let's forget Sarah. As much as we can. You decided to talk yet? I know you won't get tired of trying."

I THOUGHT YOU WERE A PATIENT MAN.

"Sarah's been trying my patience for two years now, with this writing lark. Anyway, as I said, let's forget her. It's your turn to try now."

I'LL TRY HARDER IF YOU TRY HARDER.

He smiled. "You'll try harder anyway. I know. So let's see." He took a file out of one of his drawers. "Right. 'Sally was there. Dad was there.' Now, let's think about Sally, shall we? Your mum's told me a lot about her. You two were very close, weren't you?"

I THOUGHT WE WERE GOING TO TALK ABOUT DAD.

"No. Sally."

I sighed. Felt my heart beginning to pound again. I just couldn't control it.

"Were you close, Tanya?"

I nodded.

"You loved her?"

I smiled. It was a crazy smile. I felt crazy. It was all damn crazy.

"What's funny?"

YOU SOUND LIKE MY PSYCHIATRIST.

"What was funny, Tanya?"

I'VE GOT TO SEE HIM ON FRIDAY.

"Think about Sally."

NO.

"Why not?"

I smiled.

"Did your dad push her down the stairs, Tanya?"

ARE YOU A POLICEMAN?

"No, I'm your step-father."

I DON'T WANT A STEP-FATHER.

"You want to run round in circles, don't you? To escape. What are you running from?"

YOU'RE NOT MY PSYCHIATRIST.

He sighed. "Come on, Tanya. Take control."

I'M NOT DRIVING A CAR.

"You're not trying."

YOU DON'T TRY WITH SARAH.

"Are we getting anywhere?"

YOU MADE ME SICK THE OTHER DAY.

"Yesterday."

YES.

"Why did I make you sick? What were you thinking about?"

YOU SHOULD BE A PSYCHIATRIST. YOU'D BE A GOOD ONE.

"You were thinking about Sally, weren't you? And what happened."

NO.

"I think you were. Tell me, then. What happened? What happened when you were upstairs, Tanya?"

SHE WAS THERE WITH HIM. That had been going to be my sentence.

"What was he doing?"

Did it matter? Did it really matter? Of course, because they thought. They thought what I had told them. I had told them.

HE WAS TOUCHING HER.

"Was he?"

He said that almost as if he didn't believe me. It shocked me. I looked down at my hands.

"Then what happened?"

I suddenly realized then. I suddenly realized that he didn't believe me. He didn't believe me. He'd heard the story before. He'd heard it. But they had to believe it. They had to. Everyone. They had to believe it. But what if they didn't? If they didn't? I suddenly started to panic.

"Tanya."

Sweat. Pulse. Heart. Sweat. Pulse. Heart. Beat. Beat. Beat.

"Tanya. Take control. It's all right. You can trust us."

But I couldn't. I couldn't. I couldn't trust anyone. I had to run. Get away.

He was suddenly in front of the door, though. Stopping me.

"No, Tanya. No more running."

"Leave me alone," I croaked. Something coming up from my throat. I coughed. In my panic. I

79

grappled with the figure in front of me. But he was strong. Too strong.

"You've got nowhere to run to, Tanya."

"Get out. Get out my way." It hurt. To speak. It hurt. It wasn't me talking, though. It was someone else a long, long way away.

"And what if I don't? You're going to calm down, aren't you? Face it. You're going to take deep breaths. Take deep breaths, Tanya."

"Let me go."

"You're talking."

"Let me go."

"Why?"

"You don't know."

"Where will you go?"

"To the church."

He moved out of my way. I slammed the front door shut and ran. I didn't stop running till I reached the church. I yanked the door open and went inside. I leant against the wall. Petrified. But free. No one was there. No one was there. No one was after me. I could speak but I didn't tell him. I didn't tell him. Dear God, no.

My throat was sore. I coughed. It was dry. I sat on a chair. But I couldn't stay still. I had to keep moving. Looking behind. Scared someone was there. That monster. Lurking in every corner. Ready to grab me. And then what? He'd be ugly. He'd grab my throat. I told you not to talk, he'd say. I told you not to talk. And then he'd have a knife. And dig it in me. Because I could talk. He wouldn't stop digging it in me. He'd cut me into pieces. Christ. Christ. Christ. Save me. Save me. Save me.

"Save me." My scream echoed back to my ears.

*

"It's all right, Tanya." Mum appeared out of nowhere. "It's all right. The doctor's here. He'll give you something."

"Tanya?" It was that silvery-haired man. "Take deep breaths, Tanya. It's all right. Like a nightmare. You'll want some sleep. I'll give you a little shot. It won't hurt."

He pulled my trousers half down. I felt the prick of the injection. Then I clung on to Mum.

"D'you think you can walk home or shall I get your dad to fetch the car?" The doctor spoke.

"I think we need the car," Mum said.

"All right. I'll go back and talk to your husband."

"Thank you."

I clung on to Mum like a chimpanzee on to its mother. She'd been sent to save me, that's what I thought. She'd been sent to save me.

"It's all right, darling," she soothed. "It's all right. No one's after you. No one at all. You're safe with us. You're safe with us."

"Can I talk?" The words croaked.

"Yes. I think you can."

"Why?"

"Because it's about time, that's why. I couldn't help you like Gerry's helped you, Tanya. I couldn't. It was my fault." She cried.

I stroked her hair. "I love you."

"I love you too."

I felt sleepy. My eyes were heavy. I vaguely remembered Gerry putting a blanket over me and carrying me to the car. But that's all I remembered. Nothing else. Nothing else. Only the warmth of his carrying me. I felt like a baby again. In my father's arms.

Chapter Fifteen

When I eventually woke the next day the sun was beaming into my bedroom. Someone had drawn my curtains and I could see the blue sky.

I was puzzled about the time until I looked at my clock. It was three-thirty in the afternoon. I felt relaxed. Still half asleep. I lay there slowly remembering what had happened. It all came in bits and pieces at first. Then I actually remembered that I had spoken. I tried it again. Coughing at first.

"Hello. Hello." My voice was quiet but they were words. Real words. I felt glad. Very glad. But so sleepy still. I closed my eyes.

"Tanya."

The soft voice reached into my dreams. The smiling face of Sarah greeted me. "It's five o'clock. You lazy toad."

I smiled.

"How you feeling?" She sat on the side of my bed.

I was going for my notepad. Forgetting. Forgetting what I could do. But Sarah stopped me. Made me remember. She put her hand over mine.

"Can you talk?"

I tried. "Yes."

"The doctor said you're not to talk much until you've seen a specialist. Only a few words at a time."

I nodded.

"Dad's going to bring you some soup up in a minute. So you just stay there."

"All right."

"I'm just going down to help with the dinner. And here, I bought you this. It's a good book. You'll enjoy it."

The book was called *Flowers in the Attic*.

"Thank you."

She laughed. "You sound like a dirty old man. Oh, here's Dad."

"Did you ring the bell, madam?" Gerry came in carrying a tray. "Cor, it's all right for some. Sleeping all day. And being waited on. Here you are. Sit up. Soup. Bread. And when you've finished I'll make you some scrambled egg."

"Thanks."

"Doesn't she sound like a dirty old man, Dad?"

"So would you if you hadn't talked for two years."

"How come you always sound like a dirty old man, then?"

"Cheeky so and so. All right then, Tanya? Mum will be home soon. I'll bring the egg up in ten minutes. And I'll tell the others they can come in and see you."

"Thanks."

"Rest your voice. Don't say too much."

"I've told her, Dad. She knows."

"Right, we'll get on with the dinner."

I was left alone to eat my soup. I took it slowly because my throat was sore. I felt more awake, though. Not so sleepy. My whole body ached, though. As if I'd just run a marathon or something.

83

Jason came in and talked a while. Then Gerry came up with my scrambled egg. I felt very loved, you know. By everyone. I suddenly realized how much everyone cared. Not only Mum and Jason. Gerry as well. Sarah. Clive. He came up with a bunch of flowers from the garden. He put them in a pot and stood them on my bedside table.

"There, it looks just like a hospital now."

"Thanks."

"You sound like a frog."

Well, I'd never been called a frog before. A dirty old man, yes. But not a frog. I smiled to myself. When I was alone again. I smiled to myself. So I can talk. What now? Fear came back. I didn't want to lose what I'd found. So, what would I do? Now. What would I do? Would they all leave me alone now that I could talk? Would they all leave me alone? Was that the end of it? I wondered. The monster wasn't there. I felt safe in this house. But I remembered the man. That dreadful man. I remembered what he'd said. It was all clear in my mind. I'll know if you can talk. I'll know if you can talk. He'll know. So what will he do? I shivered. I'll know if you tell anyone. I'll know if you tell anyone. Think of your mother. Think of Jason. You don't want to be the cause of their death as well. Do you? Do you? No. No. No.

I turned in my bed. Pulled the sheets up over my head. "Go away," I whispered. "Go away."

I went downstairs in my dressing gown when Mum came home. We sat together on the couch looking through their wedding album. Gerry had to go out at seven on a house visit. Clive went round to a friend's and Sarah was in her bedroom writing. So, it was just Jason, Mum and I. We didn't have the telly on because there wasn't much on. We spent a quiet evening together. It was nice and peaceful. Just us together, like it used to be. I wasn't wishing that it could always be like that, though. I didn't want to go back. To not have my new family. Especially now, now that I could talk. I suppose I realized how much I needed Gerry. A man. A father figure. I realized how such Jason needed him. And Mum too. It all added up. We all needed each other and that was nice. If only I could forget that man. If only he wasn't stinging my every movement. If only I could get the fear out of my soul. If only. If only.

The next day Gerry took me to a local hospital to see a specialist about my throat. The doctor examined me and put this long tube-like thing down my throat. But he seemed pleased. He said for me to take it easy at first and he gave me a prescription for some liquid to gargle with each day.

I was talking more and more. It was like a game at first. Everyone was so pleased. They all kept laughing at me. And I felt easier somehow, because I thought if only I could live with the thought of that man I'd be OK. I didn't think I'd have any more hassle from anyone. I'd done it. I was talking again.

"Well," the silver-haired doctor said. "Congratulations."
  "Thank you."
  "How d'you feel?"
  "All right."

"What d'you think made you talk?"

"Gerry."

"Your step-dad?"

"Yes."

"So now we can get down to things."

"I'm all right now, I can talk."

"But we have to find the reasons, don't we?"

"It doesn't matter, does it?"

"What were you scared about? Before I gave you the injection? What were you frightened for?"

I swallowed hard.

"Do you remember?"

"It doesn't matter, does it?"

"I think it matters to your mother and step-father. And to me. So, can you tell me?"

"No."

"Why?"

"It's not important."

"OK, let's go back to the day your sister was killed."

"I don't want to not talk again."

"Good. That's the first step. Sally was her name, wasn't it?"

"Yes."

"What happened, Tanya?"

"I've told everyone this a thousand times. My real father was sent to prison for it."

"But he always insisted he was innocent."

"He couldn't tell another story, could he?"

"Can you?"

"I thought if I could talk it would be the end of all this."

"You see, I think you've got a problem. Deep inside of you. About that day. I think you're frightened. Of something. Someone. You tell me."

It would have been so easy to tell him. A good part of me wanted to. But if I told him, then what would happen? Everyone would know. Everyone. That man would know.

I said nothing.

"Just tell me yes or no. Did your father kill your sister? Yes or no, that's all I'm asking."

I struggled. But as long as I didn't tell him the truth, that would be all right. I struggled with the word.

"No." No. No. No.

"Thanks, Tanya. Are you going to come to see me next Friday?"

I nodded.

"Good. Same time. I'll see you then."

Chapter Sixteen

I didn't feel happy. The excitement from talking had worn off. I sat in my bedroom most of the weekend. Being rude, may be. But Gerry was busy anyway. Perhaps he didn't really notice. I felt bogged down. Weighted. Everything seemed to be going on around me again and I had no part in it. Anyway, I didn't really want a part. I felt too bad. I was short with Jason and not talkative to Sarah.

They all went to church on Sunday morning except Clive and me.

I was in my bedroom listening to records. Clive came in without knocking. He looked around my room and then sat on my window-sill.

"What's wrong, Tanya?"

"Nothing."

"Pull the other one."

"You didn't knock."

"No. I'm bad-mannered."

"What d'you want?"

"You can tell me, you know. I can keep secrets."

"I have nothing to tell."

"Dad's watching you."

"So?"

"You're being rude again."

"So?"

"Don't you care?"

"Just leave me. I want to be alone."

"I go like you when I feel guilty about something. When I've done something wrong, you know."

"Well, I don't feel guilty."

"What've you done?"

"Nothing."

"I'm sure you have."

"You're very clever then, to read my mind."

"I take after Dad like that."

"Please will you leave me, Clive, I want to be alone."

"I just came to warn you about Dad. He doesn't like secrets. He likes everything to be in the open."

"Well, thanks for telling me."

"OK. I'm going."

He went. I looked at the closed door. For a long time I stared at that. For a long time.

Guilty? Who's guilty? That monster. Wherever he was. Why, I couldn't tell. Suddenly I laughed. "Stupid bitch." He was right, of course. Very right. Guilt erodes. My guilt. My erosion. Well, that was up to me, no one else. That was up to me.

Chapter Seventeen

The last thing I felt like doing the next day was going to work. I wouldn't have gone, if it had been just left to me. I wouldn't have gone. But Mum got me up early. She packed my lunch. Gerry was up waiting to take me to work. It was all arranged. I was going to work.

I sat in the front of the truck next to Gerry. I felt nervous. About starting work. I felt too depressed to do anything. But I was going and I couldn't do anything about it.

He dropped me outside the shop.

"Good luck," he said.

"Bye."

"I'll pick you up tonight."

I hated it. Every minute. It was stifling hot and sweaty. I felt claustrophobic. Stared at. Closed in. I managed the pressing all right. I was just doing trousers, but it was so boring. I felt like crying at lunchtime and made my mind up that I would never work there again. Never. I definitely wasn't going back there. It made me feel too trapped. I wanted to go home. All the time. I wanted to go home. The day dragged. Minute by minute. Hour by hour. Slow. So slow. All the trousers were the same. You did the same thing. Time and time again. I didn't talk. I didn't talk to anyone. I hardly noticed who else was working there. It was just dreadful.

When five o'clock came I didn't say goodbye to anyone. I just grabbed my handbag and jacket and rushed out. Trying to stop my tears from coming.

Gerry was there waiting. "How did it go, then?"

I cried. I couldn't help it.

"What's wrong, love?"

"I hate it. I'm not going back."

"But, darling, it's only your first day. What are the other young ones like?"

"I hate it. I'm not going back."

"Could you do the work?"

"Of course I could. It's easy."

"Well, that's half the battle, isn't it?"

"It's so boring."

"The first day is always bad. It'll be better tomorrow."

"No, I'm not going back."

"Mike's a lovely man."

"Let's go home."

"You've got to give it longer than a day, love." He started the engine.

I knew I couldn't give it longer than a day. I wasn't going back.

We drove home in silence.

I felt better in the safety of my bedroom. I lay on my bed. I was knackered. I closed my eyes and went to sleep. Mum woke me at seven. She sat on the side of my bed.

"How d'you feel? Gerry said you weren't too keen."

"I'm not working there."

"Maybe a full-time job is too much at the moment. I don't know."

"I'm not going back tomorrow."

"Won't you try?"

"No."

"Were you depressed?"

"Yes."

"Was that the trouble?"

"I just hated it."

"Give it another try, Tanya. Tomorrow."

"I can't."

She sighed.

"I can't. I can't. I can't."

"All right. All right. Come down for your dinner. It's in the oven."

"Where's Gerry?"

"Working in his office. Come on."

I finished my dinner. In the kitchen, alone. I was just going up the stairs again when Gerry came out of his office.

"Tanya."

I stopped. Turned round.

"Come in here. I want a word."

A word? What did that mean? I'd had a word before. I remembered only too well. I followed him back into his office, though. Sat on my normal seat. Waited.

"I want you to go back to work again, Tanya. Give it another go, tomorrow."

It was incredible. One thing over and another thing begins. With him. Gerry. It didn't seem possible. He seemed to be like a leech clinging on my back. And I couldn't shake him off. What could I say? In argument. What could I say? Could I scream? No. No. No. I'm not going back there. Could I shout and rage?

"Can I go part-time?" I tried. The only way I knew

how. "I don't know if I can cope with full-time work. Not yet."

"The doctor said you should be able to cope with it. No. I don't think it would be a good idea if you went part-time. No."

"The doctor doesn't know everything."

"Well, it's up to you to tell him."

"I don't know who is my doctor, you or him."

He smiled. "I don't think I'm quite qualified."

"Is that all you want?"

"I've been giving you a bit of grace over the weekend. It won't go on."

"Vets are meant to be gentle with animals, but they're not like that with humans, are they? They're hard with humans. Stony hard."

"I'm sorry if you've got the impression that I'm that way inclined. I didn't think so."

"Well, you are."

"You'll get used to it." He winked at me, half smiling. "See you later."

I slammed my bedroom door shut. Angry. Angry with him. He was winning, you see. Winning. All the time. And I was losing. Losing. Losing. Well, he wouldn't get me. Not all of me. He wouldn't get me.

There was a knock on my door. Sarah came in. "Tanya, d'you want to come to the Youth Club tonight?"

I shook my head.

"Oh Tansy, come on. You can't stay in here all night."

"Don't worry. He's giving me grace."

"It's not that. It's you. Come on. It'll make you forget about work. Kath said she'd take us in the truck so we won't have to cycle. She'll pick us up at ten or

93

Dad will. Oh, come on, Tansy. I could throttle you. You've been moping all weekend."

I wondered. I didn't feel tired any more anyway. Should I go?

"Someone who works where you're working goes there. He doesn't work on Mondays, that's why you didn't see him today. But perhaps you could get to know him a bit. He's a great guy. His name's Chris. He's the son of Robin, the leader. Oh come on, I'll drag you there if you don't say yes. I'll tie you up and bundle you in the truck."

I couldn't help smiling. She seemed so agitated.

"Yes? Tanya?"

"OK." I gave in. It couldn't be as bad as work. And besides, I felt like getting out of Gerry's way. "What shall I wear?"

"Your white trousers and a blouse. I'm just wearing this, but everyone knows I'm scruffy. Well done. I'll tell your mum. I'll see you downstairs." She'd got out the door when she popped her head back in again. "Don't forget to clean your teeth. You never know what might happen."

I still wasn't sure if I really wanted to go. But I washed, changed and didn't forget to clean my teeth. Perhaps it wouldn't be so bad. I'd never been to a Youth Club before. It could be fun. Fun? Is that what I deserved. I wondered. Thought of God. In a flash I thought of God. He'd forgive me. If I repented. Well, whatever that meant. Perhaps it meant to tell the truth. I shrugged. Went downstairs.

Mum and Sarah were waiting in the kitchen. "You ready, Tanya?" Mum asked.

"Yeah."

"Say bye to Gerry then."

"No."

"Oh, leave it. Come on, let's go."

Mum and I followed Sarah out.

Chapter Eighteen

It didn't take long to reach the club, which was situated back from a fairly main road, down a country track. I climbed out with Sarah and kissed Mum goodbye.

"Have fun."

"See you later," Sarah shouted, waving.

The club doors were open and Sarah went through. I followed her.

"Hello, Mary," Sarah spoke to a fat, motherly-looking woman who was standing at a desk in the entrance hall. "My step-sister's come. I'll pay for her. Visitor, isn't it? Fifty pence?"

"Give me thirty and we'll call it quits."

"Oh thanks, Mary. You're gorgeous."

"Hello, love, what's your name?" The woman was speaking to me.

"Tanya."

"Write your name and address down in the visitors' book. Just there."

"Is Robin here?" Sarah asked.

"Somewhere."

"And Chris?"

"Yes."

"Tanya's working with Chris."

"Is she? Is your dad over your part-time work yet?"

"Mary, it's amazing, he actually wants to read one of my books. Fancy that, eh. It must be this married life getting to him. For the better, I might say."

"Will he like it? That's the thing."

"I can always pray. I've given him my last one."

"You haven't given it to me to read yet."

"When I'm famous, Mary, when I'm famous."

"You won't want to know us lot when you're famous."

"Would I forget you, Mary? Come on, Tanya. I'll show you around."

There was a large lounge bar going off from the entrance hall. With easy chairs and tables. Sarah spoke to a few people and introduced me to a few more. There was a sweet bar and a record player. There was a Police LP on when we went in, with a group of boys crowded round.

"Hello, vet's daughter," one shouted out.

"Hello, policeman's son," Sarah retaliated.

"Hey, Sarah. Here, I owe you. Catch." A tall boy with ginger hair threw a cigarette at Sarah. She caught it, looking a bit guiltily at me.

"I only smoke up here. Keep it quiet, eh?"

I smiled. She was a right one. She took a light from a girl. It was weird, seeing her smoke. It just didn't look right somehow.

"D'you want a Coke or something? I'll treat you."

"OK."

We went up to the bar.

"Hello, trouble," a man said.

"This is Tanya, my step-sister. You have to watch what you do when he's around, Tanya. He's one of those fuzz people."

"Hello, Tanya, nice to meet you. I hope you're not going to go the same way as your sister here. She's a right trouble-maker."

97

"No, I'm not."

"Thinks she can write. We try to humour her."

"Oh, very funny, Dick. Give me two Cokes."

"Please."

"Please, my darling, Dick, please."

"That'll be forty pence."

"Where's Robin?"

"In the big hall, I think."

"OK. See yer later. Come on, Tans."

We went through some swing doors to another hall. It was much larger than the lounge and quite a bit was going on. There were two table tennis tables up, a trampoline and some boys doing weight-lifting.

"There's Robin."

I followed Sarah over to a thin man who was watching the trampolining.

"Hello, Robin."

"Oh, hello, gutsy. How are you? Recovered now, have you? Everything rosy at home?"

"Not bad. Not bad. This is Tanya. I told you."

"Oh, this is Tanya. Well, I've heard a lot about you, love. Glad you came."

"She's working with Chris at the cleaners. She hasn't met him yet but I'm going to introduce them."

"Oh, you're working at Suedette, are you?"

"I started today."

"Chris has his day off today. He'll be there tomorrow, though. You can try to cheer him up for me. He's been in a right mood since Sue finished with him."

"I'll cheer him up," Sarah said. "Where is he?"

"Out the back mucking about with his motorbike. I don't think he feels sociable somehow."

"He soon will, don't worry."

"Tanya, are you any good at writing poetry?" he asked.

I looked at Sarah.

"She's brilliant."

"Can't she talk for herself?"

"I can write poetry, yeah." I felt myself blush.

"Come with me and I'll give you an entry form. We've got a competition going."

"See that door down there, Tanya?" Sarah said.

"Yeah."

"I'll be in there."

"OK."

I tentatively followed Robin out of the large hall.

"Have you met Tanya?" he asked Mary.

"Yes. We've met."

"We've got to impress her tonight. We want her to come back again."

"I think she will."

"Come on then, love. I'll show you my office."

He unlocked a door and we went into a small box-shaped room.

"Right, what am I looking for? An entry form. D'you read much?"

"Quite a bit."

"First prize is a ten pound book token. So that could be handy for you. Here you are. You write your poem on here and hand it in to me or one of the leaders. It can be about anything."

"OK."

"And don't look so worried. We're not going to eat you."

I smiled. I liked him. He was all right. In fact, the whole place wasn't bad. It had a good atmosphere. Relaxed.

I crossed the hall feeling slightly conscious of being the new girl and went through the door Sarah had pointed out to me. I found her sitting on a wooden crate watching a fair-haired boy work on a motorbike.

"Oh hi, Tansy. Meet Chris. Chris, Tansy."

The boy stood. He was quite tall and had large blue eyes.

"Hi. Sorry I can't shake your hand. Unless you want to be covered in oil."

"That's OK, hi."

"How d'you like living with this one here, then? Famous author to be. It must be quite an experience."

I smiled. Wasn't sure what to say. I felt kind of awkward.

"It's great living with me, isn't it, Tanya?"

"It's not bad."

"I hear you started at Suedette today."

"Yeah."

"You'll be on the press next to me. How d'you like it?"

"A bit boring."

"That's 'cause I wasn't there. It's always boring when I'm not around. Isn't it, Sarah?"

"Of course, darling. The world wouldn't survive without you."

"Oh, I know that."

"Want a fag?"

"Have you actually got some then?"

"Cheeky sod. Of course I have." Sarah rummaged in her jacket pocket and brought out a packet of cigarettes. She gave one to Chris and lit one herself.

"Well, I don't know if this thing's going to work," Chris said, taking a puff at his cigarette.

"Probably not, if you've been working on it."

"Thanks. I love you too."

"Your dad said you're feeling unsociable. You'll make a good pair with Tanya. She's feeling unsociable too."

"For different reasons, no doubt."

"That's what everyone's been saying."

"It's true. Anyway, you're not going to be stuck in here all night. Come and have a game of darts with us."

"I might consider it."

"Of course you'll consider it. With two gorgeous females such as ourselves."

"How could I resist?"

"You just couldn't."

"I'll have to clean up first. I've had enough of working on this thing for the night anyway."

"OK, we'll see you out there."

"Hey, Tanya."

I turned round as we were leaving him.

"Nice to meet you."

I smiled.

"You see," Sarah said. "You're in there."

"What?"

"You know."

"Don't be daft."

"I know these things. Come on, let's go and get the darts."

We played the game one to twenty. I'd never played darts before but I wasn't that bad at it. Chris came out and I must admit to being quite impressed with him. He was good-looking anyway. We finished one to twenty and suddenly Sarah disappeared, so I was left alone with Chris. I felt a right twit because I just didn't know what to say.

"Play 301, Tanya?"

"301?"

"Start straight in, end with a double. First one to 301. It's easy. You're good at darts. You might even beat me."

"All right then."

"I'll do the taking away."

He chalked our names up on the board and gave us both 301.

"You start."

I didn't win. I couldn't get a double at the end. It was a good game, though. We both sat down afterwards and I didn't feel so awkward with him.

"How d'you like your new life, then?"

"It's all right."

"I'm glad you're working at Suedette. We'll be able to have a chat. As long as we get our work done Mike doesn't mind."

"I hated it today."

"First day's awful, isn't it? There's a disco up here Friday, are you coming?"

I shrugged.

"Sarah will come."

"I might do."

"Can you dance?"

"Sort of, I s'pose."

"I'll teach you."

"All right."

"Wanna game of table tennis?"

"I can't play."

"I'll teach you that as well, come on."

*

The night went. As quick as that it went. I enjoyed it. Mainly spent with Chris, of course. We had fun at table tennis. He was nice. Really gentle. I didn't think he fancied me or anything, though. We just had fun. Then we went in the lounge again, where we joined Sarah and a group of girls and boys. I didn't do much talking but listened to everyone else. They all seemed really friendly, though, and one girl offered me a cigarette. Which, actually, I was tempted to take because they were all smoking, but I decided against it. My throat felt too dry as it was. Anyway then Sarah looked at her watch and motioned to me that it was time to go. Then she put out her cigarette and took from her pocket a breath-freshener spray which she sprayed in her mouth. I really giggled at her. She was a right one.

"See you tomorrow, Tanya," Chris said. "I'll cheer you up."

"And she'll cheer you up," Sarah said. "Just right, that is. Just right. See you. Bye, everyone."

"Bye, vet's daughter."

"Bye, policeman's son."

Robin was standing talking to Mary in the entrance hall.

"You off?" he said.

"Yep. Chris is all right."

"I noticed. See you Wednesday?"

"Yeah."

"Enjoy it, Tanya?"

"Yes, thanks."

"Just don't let them get you into any bad habits. Like smoking, for instance."

"I won't."

"Take care. See you Wednesday."

"Bye."

"Bye."

Gerry was waiting outside for us. Sarah and I climbed in the back of the truck.

"All right, girls?"

"Guess what, Dad."

I knew what she was going to say.

"It's not true. Shut up."

"Well, let's say she made a friend."

"Oh yeah."

"Male as well. That was a good bit of fixing up, wasn't it? I'm good at playing Cupid. He works at Suedette too. He wasn't there today but he will be tomorrow. She definitely wants to go to work now."

"It's all lies." I settled back in the seat but all the same felt quite chuffed. I suppose I did like him. Although I wasn't sure if I fancied him. I'd never fancied anyone before, so how did I know? But I s'pose the thought of work didn't seem quite so bad now that he was going to be there.

We arrived home, and Sarah and I went in while Gerry put the truck away. Mum had our cups ready for a night-time drink. She was watching the News. Sarah went in and told her all about Chris. I thumped her one.

"It's all lies, isn't it, Tanya?" Gerry came in. "She's stirring it again."

"Yeah, she is."

"But anyway, you had a good time."

"It's good there, Mum. I'm going in for a poetry competition. A ten pound book token is first prize."

"And I'm winning that," Sarah said.

"There's a disco on Friday."

"We're going, aren't we, Tanya?"

"I might." I half joked. I knew I wanted to go really.

The phone rang then. Gerry went out to answer it, and I sat down next to Mum.

"How d'you feel, Tanya?"

"Knackered. But all right."

"Good. I'm glad you went tonight. Are they nice people?"

"They seem it."

"So what about work tomorrow?"

"I'll try again. It'll be better because of Chris being there. He's the leader's son. Robin, the leader, he's all right."

"Good."

Good.

Good.

I felt good.

Good.

I felt absolutely fine.

Chapter Nineteen

Work improved. It definitely did improve over the next few days. It was much better with Chris working beside me. We had conversations. About all sorts of things. Then we had races to see how many pairs of trousers we could press in an hour. Of course, we had to be careful to press them properly, but it made the time go faster. I began talking to a girl called Angie who was a year older than me. She wore heavy make-up and really fashionable clothes. She was quite nice, though. Then there was an older girl there who was manageress. Now, I really took to her. She reminded me of Sarah in a way, mainly because she didn't wear any make-up. She was really helpful and taught me how to serve the customers. We had our lunch break together too and she always made me a cup of coffee and lent me her paper to read.

Mike was out quite a bit of the time, but when he was in he'd wink at me or prod me in the stomach. Or stop and chat. Usually about church or something. Asking how Clive was, because he didn't go to church any more. And then there was Mike's father in the mornings. Talking and being generally friendly. It all made things seem so much better.

I had to ask for Friday morning off because of having to go to see the psychiatrist, but Mike was pleasant about it. Then on Thursday I received my first pay packet. Fifty pound I actually took home. I was right chuffed when I got in Gerry's truck on Thursday night after we'd just got paid, because I hadn't really been expecting that much.

"Fifty pound, I've got," I said.

"Before tax?"

"After tax."

"That's good."

"I'm rich."

"You can start saving for a car."

"A car?"

"Yeah. I can teach you to drive."

"Really?" I hadn't thought of that.

"Yes."

"In this truck?"

"Why not?"

"Well, it is brand new, practically."

"I have faith in you, Tanya."

"Cor. Hey, but Gerry."

"Mm?"

"I was wondering how much to give Mum for keep. I thought half. D'you think that would be all right? Twenty-five pound."

"Offer it to her and see what she says."

"D'you think it's enough, though?"

"Yeah, it's enough."

"OK then, I'll see what she says."

We arrived home then. At quarter past five on the dot. I felt happy. I wasn't thinking about going to see the psychiatrist the next day. It was far from my mind. No one had been getting at me that week, and apart from my first day at work everything had gone well.

It came to me that night. After Mum and Gerry had been in to see me. Gerry had said I wouldn't have to get up until nine because my appointment wasn't until ten. When they'd gone and I was alone in the darkness I really remembered. The weekly visit. Well, great. It would be OK. Nothing to get in a hassle about. No one had been hassling me. Not even Gerry. I was working. I was happy.

God forgives.

God forgives.

God forgives.

I didn't want to think about it. I tried to push it from my mind.

God wouldn't forgive you.

You must be punished.

I giggled. That crazy giggle, like before. Why worry? No hassle. No hassle. It was him anyway. That man. That monster. But somehow it didn't stick then. It just didn't stick. What man? What monster? How long could I kid myself? How long? He knew, the doctor. He'd asked me if my father had killed her. I'd said no. What now? Tomorrow. What would happen tomorrow? God. God. God. But I wasn't nervous. I wasn't worried. I felt safe in the house. Gerry was a Christian. He had God on his side and God forgives.

Chapter Twenty

I'd begun sweating in the car going over to the hospital. My seat belt seemed to be pressing me further and further into the seat. I felt breathless.

It was hell waiting. And then he came out and called me in.

"Hello, Tanya."

"Hello."

"How are you?"

"All right."

"You're working now, then."

I wondered how he knew.

"D'you like it?"

"It's all right."

"Coping?"

"Yes."

"Happy?"

"Yes."

He seemed to be studying my file. I sat twiddling my fingers.

"Tanya."

I looked at him.

"This isn't going to be nice for you, but we're going to have to talk about something."

I smiled. "I'm happy. I'm well. I'm talking. Nothing's wrong with me any more."

"You know what we have to talk about, don't you?"

"I thought you were meant to make people better."

"Even so."

"OK. What?"

"July the fifth."

"Yeah. So?"

"Your father didn't murder your sister, yet he was put away for it."

"Maybe I was lying when I said no. Muddled. I don't know. It's all over and done with."

"But it's not, is it?"

"Look, I'm better."

"Your step-father and I have suggested that now you're settled in at work you have ten minutes with him each day again. It seems to have done you good."

"Oh, so now you're conspiring, are you? Who are you? The C.I.D. or something."

"No. D'you think we should be?"

"What's that meant to mean?"

"What does it mean to you?"

"Nothing. Just nothing."

"If your father didn't kill your sister, the question is, who did?"

"Look. I don't have to sit here and take this. You're not helping me. I'm going."

I left. Quickly. Got out. Not frenzied, though. Still amazingly calm. I didn't even slam his door.

"Let's go," I said to Gerry.

"Finished?"

"Come on."

"Here's the key to the truck. I'll meet you there."

"Why aren't you coming?"

"I want to talk to the doctor."

"Oh yeah? So that's your game, is it?"

"No game, love."

"Well, you have been conspiring. You think the same thing, do you? As him. You're trying to trap me. Well, it won't work because I'm not that stupid."

"Tanya, I can't talk to you here. We're disturbing people. Go to the truck."

"Well, thanks. I really thought I could trust you. It seems that I was wrong." I grabbed the keys from his hand and made for the exit. Angry. So damn angry.

I was waiting in the truck fifteen minutes. I timed it. So they had fifteen minutes of confab. I was absolutely livid when he got in the truck.

"Put your seat belt on, love."

"Don't call me love."

"All right. All right. You'll pay the fine if you get caught."

"And what was all that crap about you teaching me to drive? That was all crap, wasn't it? Just to get me on your side. Well, it won't work because I'm not fooled. I never will be."

"And do you think you can live with your secrets?"

"I think I can do without you, thanks very much."

He said nothing more. We drove home in silence. I slammed the truck door but had to wait at the back door because he had the key. I slammed every door in the house which I could slam. Opening them again to slam them again. I thumped noisily up the stairs. I knocked a pot of flowers over which was on the landing. When I got in my room I had to restrain myself from smashing a window. I had to do something, though. I had to do something to show him that he wouldn't win. I went into the bathroom. I destroyed everything in there. Poured all the bubble bath away. Crushed all the bath cubes. Pushed all the toothpaste over the loo seat. Put the loo rolls down the loo. Smashed all the bottles I could find in the bath. I destroyed that place and loved every minute of it. They'd ruined my happiness, you see. Every time I found a bit of happiness they had to ruin it. And I hated them for it. Really hated them.

I left the bathroom. Went to my room. Trembling, I was. Trembling. Tears of rage running down my face. I took deep breaths. Oddly, I felt like a cigarette. Then I remembered Sarah had given me hers on Wednesday night to look after. I found them in my handbag. It was a relief to see them there. I lit one, took a puff; coughed. Took another puff; it hurt my throat, but I persevered. By the end of that cigarette I was ready for another one. So lit it. I sat on my bed smoking. Imbeciles, I thought. They're all fucking imbeciles. They don't know anything. Nothing at all. None of them do. None of them.

I stayed in my room until half past eleven, then I decided I'd walk to work. I knew how to get there. I took my handbag and went out the front door. I didn't tell him. Why the hell should I?

It took me forty-five minutes to walk. I stopped at a sweet shop on the way and bought a bag of crisps, a Mars bar and a can of Coke for my lunch. I felt calmer to be out on my own. Away from it all.

Chris was having his lunchbreak when I got in, so I sat in the kitchen with him. I smoked another cigarette.

"Christ!" he said. "What side of the bed did you get out of this morning? And you don't smoke."

"Actually I do. As from about an hour ago."

"Should I ask how it went?"

He knew where I was going that morning, because I'd told him.

"Terribly. Sodding awfully. I feel like going. Anywhere. Just anywhere. A million miles away."

"That bad?"

"Yep."

"Wanna talk about it?"

"That's funny, as it happens. Wanna talk? You know."

"Yeah. Sorry."

I sighed. "I really want to go, Chris."

"Run?"

"Why d'you have to call it run?"

"Psychology. I get it from Dad. What you running from?"

"Everyone."

"Everyone but you."

"It's hassle all the time. Just hassle. Everyone has to hassle. They're not satisfied otherwise."

He sighed. "I don't know the half of it, but . . ."

"Yeah?"

"I know they care."

"Care?" I smiled.

"It's true. You wouldn't be running from them."

"I think I should get angry with you."

"But you're not."

"No. I destroyed the bathroom in my anger. Christ."

"Have you cooled down now?"

"I must have."

"Can you think rationally?"

"Perhaps."

"So, think it out. You've got all afternoon. Think it out. See if it's worth it. In the long run."

"The trouble is, I don't know."

"What?"

"What could happen."

"Well, would it be something absolutely disastrous?"

"It could be. I don't know."

"Can't you ask someone?"

"Hell knows. I don't."

"Ask me."

I smiled.

"No?"

I shrugged.

"Ask my dad."

That made me think. Just a bit. It made me think.

"Would you?"

"I don't know if I could."

"It would be in absolute confidence. He'd tell no one. He's a great guy. My best friend."

I wasn't sure.

"Think about it. As I say, you've got all afternoon."

"OK, I'll think. Here, d'you want these? I don't feel like eating them."

"Keep them here. For next week."

"I'll go and start work."

"Tanya."

"Yeah."

"I am on your side, you know."

"Thanks." I meant that. With the whole of my heart. With the whole of my damn, sodding, sodding, heart.

"It's quiet in here this afternoon." Mike said. "What's wrong with everyone? All right, Tanya?"

"Yeah."

"Chris?"

"I'm all right, ta."

"Well, silence is golden, or so they say. Trousers are lovely, Tanya. You're doing a fine job."

I s'pose I calmed down during the afternoon. Calmed down enough to regret doing what I did to the bathroom. I was worried about Gerry. I was sure he wouldn't give me grace over that. I was feeling scared to go home. Not only about the bathroom but about the rest. The rest. What could I do? What should I do? It was a man. It was a man. It was a man. He threatened to kill Mum. I can't talk. He'll kill Mum. I couldn't talk. My story. My story. All the time lying in my mind. Lying to hide my guilt. But it couldn't go on. Everyone was getting too close. Getting to the core. My soul. Opened. For the first time in two years. Opened. Fresh. Alive. Did it smell good? Would it taste good? Would my chains be unlocked? Would I walk free? Or would another cage await me? A different sort of cage. It was a risk, wasn't it? A huge, great risk and I wasn't sure if I could take it.

Chris's dad. Robin. Robin. I wondered. He knew nothing. He wasn't part of me. He wouldn't hassle. He wouldn't care. He'd just take it. Take it. In confidence. In confidence. In confidence. I wondered, but I still hadn't come to a decision when five o'clock came.

Chris walked out with me. Gerry wasn't there and I was glad. But I was in a right panic about going home.

"He's not here, is he?" Chris said.

"No."

"D'you want to go for a little walk? I'm in no hurry. My train doesn't come until twenty to."

"OK."

We crossed the road and walked towards the town.

"Well, have you thought? About Dad?"

"I've thought, yeah."

"But?"

"Give me more time."

"Is it really that bad, Tanya?"

"Yeah."

"Do you want to get drunk and tell me?"

"I want to get drunk and piss off."

"Dad says that running doesn't solve anything."

"That's what my step-dad would say."

"They're right, you know."

"How come you're so mature for eighteen?"

"Growing up without a mother, I s'pose."

I looked at him. I hadn't known that.

"Yeah. She committed suicide when I was ten."

"Christ! I'm sorry."

"Oh, it's OK."

"I didn't know."

"Well, we all have our problems, don't we? Dad won't get married again, I know that. He buries himself in his work."

"Sorry, Chris. I am, really."

"Yeah."

Suddenly I felt so selfish. All my problems all the time. Always thinking about myself.

"What're you thinking about, Tanya?"

"Me, as usual."

He smiled.

"Is that funny?"

"No. Sad."

"Sometimes, I s'pose, you can make your own sadness."

"That's true. Life's what you make it."

"What about if you don't make it?"

"You drop out, don't yer."

"Do you die?"

"Inside. Yeah, I s'pose."

"Chris."

"Mm?"

"I killed someone."

"What?" He stopped walking. Half looked at me as if I was joking.

"Simple. I told you. I don't know why."

"Talk to Dad about it, Tanya. Tonight. I'll tell him you want to talk. Come up to the youth club and he'll see you in his office."

"OK."

We suddenly put our arms round each other. Hugged tightly. "Tanya."

"Mm?"

"Thanks for telling me. Dad will help you. He'll know what to do."

"Will you visit me in prison?"

"Who was it, Tanya?"

"My sister."

"Christ."

"Will you come and visit me in prison?"

"You won't go to prison. I know you won't."

"But if I do."

"I'll visit you."

"Thanks."

"You will come up tonight, won't you? You'll go home and you won't do anything daft?"

"I'll just go home. I'll see you this evening."

"D'you want me to walk you home? I will."

"No. I'll be all right."

"Be all right, Tanya. Please. Thanks for telling me."

"Thanks for listening."

"You all right to go now?"

"Yeah."

He was scared to leave me. I could tell that. And I was suddenly scared for him. For burdening him with it. I hoped he'd be all right. All the way home I hoped he'd be all right.

Chapter Twenty-One

I took a deep breath and opened the back door. No one was in the kitchen. I could hear the television but nothing else. I was frightened but knew I couldn't just go up to my room. I looked in the oven to see if there was a dinner for me and there wasn't. I tried to pluck up enough courage to go into the lounge. When I heard the lounge door open I actually jumped.

I knew it was Gerry. I didn't have to look at him. I just sensed his presence. I looked at the floor. Knowing, just knowing he was angry. He didn't speak, though. He didn't speak for what seemed like ages.

"Where've you been?"

"To work."

"I suppose it's given you time to cool down."

"I'm sorry about the bathroom."

"You are?"

I didn't say anything.

"I think you've got a few apologies to make. To your sister and brothers. To your mother. Then you'd better set to and clean the bathroom. You can replace everything you ruined tomorrow. I've written a list. After you've cleared up I want to see you in my office. And don't take too long. Even my patience isn't everlasting. And by God you've tried it today."

I went upstairs slowly. It didn't seem to matter that I'd told Chris I'd killed my sister. It didn't seem to matter. I thought if I actually told someone there would be an absolute commotion. I thought everything would happen at once. But oddly, it seemed like an anti-climax.

I knocked on Sarah's door.

"Come in."

I did so. She was sitting at her desk. She didn't seem pleased to see me. "Oh, hello."

"I'm sorry, Sarah."

"Yeah. Well. OK. I'm busy, I can't talk."

I went out. Into Clive's room. He was off with me too, although I apologized. He didn't smile. He didn't look at me. Virtually ignored me. Jason wasn't in his room. I knew he must have been downstairs with Mum. I dreaded the thought of facing Mum. I felt so ashamed and I just couldn't bear it if she was cross with me too. And Jason. The whole family. All against me. No. I couldn't bear that.

Jitters raged in my stomach as I stood outside the lounge door. But I knew I had to go in, so tried to numb myself before opening the door.

They were both sitting on the settee watching telly. Both looking gloomy. Cross. My heart sank.

"Mum?"

Hard eyes turned on me.

"Please don't be cross with me."

"I've left the cleaning stuff out on the kitchen table."

"I'm sorry. Jason, I'm sorry. I'll replace everything."

"That's hardly the point," Jason grunted.

"What d'you mean?"

"I mean, you think you're the Queen of Sheba. That you're Miss Muck. That you're the only one who matters in this house. You forget that the five of us matter. The world isn't only made up of Miss Tanya Beecham, you know."

His words hurt. Deeply. Coming from Jason, who never said a bad word about me. They hurt. I couldn't do anything, though. I couldn't say anything to either of them to make things right. I went upstairs to the bathroom. Crying. They'd left it just exactly how I'd left it. It looked awful. I didn't know where to start. My tears made it worse. I kept thinking, I'd confessed. Thinking everyone should be pleased with me. I'd confessed. Chris knew. But I hadn't confessed to Gerry. No. Perhaps I would, though. Perhaps I would. Maybe that would solve it. Solve this. This mess. Maybe they'd understand then why I had to do it. And it wasn't because I thought I was the Queen of Sheba. It was because I'd killed her. Me. My own hands. I sat on the edge of the bath. Remembering. I'd killed her. My sister. My sweet, innocent, five-year-old sister. Oh yes, he'd pushed her down the stairs, that monster, but she hadn't been killed. She was still alive. I hated her, though. Hated her because I'd seen them. Those two. Acting they were, acting like a real father and daughter. So, up on the landing, I'd attacked him with rage. In the commotion he accidentally barged against her and she fell. I rushed down the stairs. I hated her then. Nothing but rage was within me. Because he'd kissed her. Kissed her on the forehead. I'd grabbed our metal umbrella stand. Just lashed it against her head. Again and again. Again and again. Until I saw *him* standing over me, watching. Him. A friend of Dad's. I hadn't known he'd been in the house. I hadn't seen him. But he was there, watching me, that tramp-like man.

He began laughing. I remember the laugh as I was cleaning the umbrella stand. Washing the blood off it. An echoing laugh which went right through by body. I rushed upstairs just to get away from it. I found Dad quivering on the landing. My last words. The last words I spoke were, "You killed her." Then I went downstairs and the man was still there.

"He battered her over the head," he said. "I saw him do it. She wouldn't have got those injuries by falling. I'll lie for you. As long as you do something for me first."

I nodded. I nodded. Anything. I would have done anything.

"I thought I told you to clean the bathroom. Not just sit there," Gerry shouted. His voice barging into my mind. I jumped up. "Come out here." He pulled me out, on to the landing. Pushed me against the wall. "What're you doing? Thinking about yourself again? Feeling sorry for yourself? Poor Tanya, she's had such a lot to put up with. Poor Tanya. Well, don't you think I don't know what's going on inside your head? Think I can't see? Think we don't know? You're the only one suffering, are you? Poor little Tanya. You think you're the only one knowing what happened. Well, can't you get it into your head that all of us aren't exactly morons? Now, get in there and do what I said." He shoved me. I fell against the bath. His words ringing in my head. Ringing. Ringing. Ringing. But not forming. I didn't really understand them. I had no time to think. I frantically began to clean the bathroom. Clearing up all the broken glass. Washing down all the mess. Taking the loo roll out of the loo. All the time crying. Sobbing. My nose running. My eyes running. Scared to make any sense of what he'd said. But gradually I did make sense of it. I made myself think, while working. I made myself think. They knew. They knew. How? How did they know? That man. After I'd done what he said. He promised to tell no one the truth. He promised. But what's a promise to a man?

I knew it was over. It wasn't possible. I couldn't go on. I wanted to die. It hadn't worked out how I'd wanted it to. It was over. I was just a slut, that's all. A no-good slut. I'd wanted to do what I had with that man. I'd wanted to kill my sister. It was all my fault. Me. Miss Muck. Queen of Sheba. And they knew. They all knew. So, it was the end. It had to be the end. They'd been fooling me. All along they'd been fooling me. They knew I was a murderer. I wouldn't throw any more tantrums. I wouldn't act spoilt. I wouldn't hold my breath to die. I wouldn't do that. I'd make a proper job of it.

Chapter Twenty-Two

The razor blade was in the bathroom cupboard. It was a new one. Wrapped in paper. I was sweating when I took it out but I'd stopped crying. I looked at the razor. OK, so, a life for a life. God can't forgive me. God can never forgive me. I don't want him to. I want to go to hell.

It didn't hurt. Not really. It was just like ice being run over my wrist. Ice. Blood was dripping everywhere when I took the blade and cut my other wrist. Neatly. So neatly, though, I did it. I don't know why then but I suddenly started to run the bath. I wanted to die in there. I started taking my clothes off. I was going to hell. I wanted to be naked for it. Naked for my sins. Blood poured into the water, making it turn red. I took all my clothes off and climbed in. I closed my eyes.

I was fully conscious when Gerry found me. I remember telling him to go away. Then he went out and I heard him call Mum. They were all so awfully efficient about it. Getting me out of the bath. Tying tight things around my arms. They were all so efficient.

Gerry wrapped me in my dressing gown and carried me downstairs. I heard talk that the ambulance was on its way. He told me to sit. He put me on the kitchen table. "Are you cross?" I kept saying. "Are you cross?"

"No, love, of course I'm not."

"Were you?"

"Not really."

"I killed my sister, didn't I?"

"No you didn't. You killed no one. It's all in your mind, Tanya. Nasty things in your mind because nasty things have happened to you. But you'll be all right now. You'll go back to hospital for a while, but you'll be all right. It's all over. This had to come, Tanya. It had to come, love."

The ambulance came. Nice ambulance men. Mum came with me. Small, medicine-smelling ambulance. Efficiency again. To hospital. Stitched wrists. Sore, stitched wrists. I'm not dead. I'm not dead. I'm not dead. In the accident centre, lying on a high bed. Mum and Gerry either side. Mum stroking my hair. Gerry holding my hand. Nice. So nice.

"Will God forgive me?" I asked Gerry.

"What for?"

"Killing Sally."

"You didn't kill her."

"I didn't?"

"No."

"Who did?"

"Who's Sally."

"My sister."

"You've never had a sister."

"Yes, I have."

"No, you haven't. Sally was your imaginary friend. In your imagination. She wasn't a real person."

I wondered about that. But, God, she had seemed so real.

"Mum?"

"Mm?"

"There wasn't only me and Jason, was there?"

125

"Yes there was. I only had two of you."

"Who's Sally then?"

"She was your pretend sister."

"Did I kill her?"

"I think when you had the accident you lost her for a while. You thought she'd left you on purpose. So when she came back you killed her. In your mind. Only pretending. Like on television. It wasn't in real life."

"What accident?"

"Don't you remember?"

"Was it in a car?"

"That's right."

"Who was driving?"

"Your father."

I touched my face. Felt the scar tissue. Moved my hand to where my right eye should have been, but there was only a withered closed lid. It all seemed so clear then. Everything. I looked at my arms. At the white burn scars. My fingers. Pink. Scarred. I didn't have to look at my body. I knew it was the same.

"It was a fire, wasn't it?"

"Yes."

"I was trapped in the car."

"Yes."

I looked across the ward. I saw my psychiatrist.

"Gerry."

"Yes, love."

"Can I come home now? I'm better."

"A few days in hospital. That's all."

"Will you come to see me?"

"Of course I will."

My doctor came over then and Mum left with Gerry.

"Well, Tanya, what've you been doing?"

"I don't know."

"Are your wrists sore?"

"Just a bit."

"Tell me why you did it."

"Everyone knew I killed Sally, didn't they?"

"Did you kill her?"

"They say she wasn't there."

"What do you think?"

"I look like a monster, don't I?"

"You look beautiful. Especially now that you're nearly better. Anyway, now that you're well you'll be able to have plastic surgery. They can work wonders."

"How long will I have to stay in hospital for?"

"Not long."

"That man knew I'd killed her. He was laughing. All the time laughing."

"Has he stopped now?"

"I think so."

"That's good. Right, Tanya, I'm going to give you a little injection now. Then you're going for a small ambulance ride over to the unit. You'll like it there."

He gave me the injection.

"I'll see you in the morning, Tanya. You just get a good sleep. I'll call your parents in."

My parents. My parents. Mum and Dad. Mum and Gerry. Dad? I hated him. I wanted him to be dead. Dad? My real dad. I wanted him to be dead.

Mum and Gerry came back.

"All right, love?" Gerry asked. "We're going for a little ride."

"Mum?"

"Yes, Tanya."

"Tell me he's dead. Him. Tell me he's dead."

"He's not dead, love. He's in prison. But you don't have to worry. He'll never get near you again. Never."

"Will Gerry protect me?"

"Of course he will," she smiled. "He'll protect us all."

Her words were comforting. I was glad.

The porters came and wheeled me to an ambulance. Gerry and Mum came too. It was only a couple of minutes' ride. But I'd begun to get really sleepy. I didn't really remember going into the unit. I just remembered Mum and Gerry kissing me good-bye. I remembered their warmth. And thanked God for them. Somewhere in my drowsiness I thanked God for them.

Chapter Twenty-three

A nurse woke me up for breakfast in the morning. I knew I was in hospital. My mind was clear about what had happened. I still felt drowsy, though. I felt like sleeping. They gave me a different-coloured striped dressing gown to wear. It reminded me of Joseph's amazing technicolour dreamcoat. I'd seen a play about that once.

I sat around a small table with three other people. I had cornflakes and toast for my breakfast. One of the other people, a blonde-haired woman, kept staring at me. Then she put her spoon in my cornflakes and ate a spoonful. It was funny really. It made me laugh.

"Hilda," a male nurse said, "that's not your breakfast. Keep to your own."

"What's wrong with her?"

"That's none of your business."

"What's wrong with her face?"

"Hilda! I won't tell you again. Just eat your breakfast. Sorry, Tanya. Don't take any notice of her."

I s'pose she thought I looked like a monster. What I felt like at times. Scared ever since the accident to look in a mirror. I felt like withdrawing again then. That awful feeling to not be a part.

"Looks don't mean a thing, love. It's your character that counts. Build that up and you're made."

I looked at the elderly man sitting opposite me. He

winked and smiled. "People put Jesus down, didn't they? People. Huh, sod them."

I studied his grey eyes. They were old. Wise. "Your one good eye could tell a whole different story. If only you'd let it. I know, love. I've been through two wars. Take my word. Practice. It just takes practice."

I looked at the tape over my wrists. What had I done? Tried to take my life. But what else could I have done? Forget about the past. What else can I do now?

The doctor wanted to see me soon after breakfast. My doctor. The silvery-haired one. A nurse showed me to his office and she came in with me.

"Morning, Tanya."

"Morning."

"Well, how're you feeling?"

"Better, thank you."

"Had a good sleep?"

"Yes."

"Still sleepy?"

"Just a bit."

"That'll wear off. I don't think we need to give you another injection this morning."

He wrote some notes and then looked at me.

"Why did you do that, Tanya?"

"My wrists?"

He nodded.

"I thought I'd killed my sister. I wanted to go to hell."

"D'you still think you killed your sister?"

"No. It's a bit confused in my mind. But I know that I never had a sister."

"And you did no one any harm."

"No. It was so real, though."

"And was there another man involved?"

"Now I know there wasn't. But he seemed real. I thought he saw me do it. That he took me to bed with him. And said he wouldn't say anything. But I kept hearing him laugh at me."

"Did you hear voices in your head? Telling you what to do."

"No. It was just like a haze. I thought somebody would kill me for killing her."

"But, in fact, the truth was that someone nearly killed you. And in the process maimed you badly."

I looked down at my hands.

"D'you feel ashamed, Tanya?"

"It was because of what I did. The accident."

"What you did when?"

"Before. Before the accident. I knew something dreadful would happen to me, because of what I did."

"Can you remember what that was?"

"Yes."

"D'you want to tell me?"

I looked down at my hands again. "I had sex with him."

"With who?"

"My father."

"D'you feel like talking about it?"

"I don't know. Sometimes it comes back to me more than other times. But I knew something terrible would happen to me. All the time he was driving. What happened was worse than death. God was giving me my own sentence for sinning."

"You thought you deserved punishment, then?"

"Yes."

"Had it happened before, Tanya? With your father? Had he had incest with you before?"

"No. Just then."

"Did you want to have sex with him?"

I thought a long time. Silence surrounded us. And then I knew.

"No. No."

"Did you think you did?"

"Well, it takes two to tango. That's what everyone says. It takes two. I must have wanted to."

"In some circumstances the norm isn't correct, Tanya. I think you should try and understand that."

"If I didn't deserve it then why did I get like this?"

"Tell me about the car accident, Tanya. Why did you go out with him in the car? Especially after he'd done that to you?"

"When I was home I always went with him to pick Mum up from work. I didn't feel like it. I just felt like locking myself away. But I didn't want Mum to think there was anything wrong. That's why I went."

"Was he drunk?"

"Yes."

"Why was he put in prison, Tanya?"

"Because he killed a child in the accident."

"How do you feel? Talking about it now. Does it make you feel better?"

I nodded. "I s'pose so."

"And can you accept yourself as you are? You know you were scarred. Can you accept yourself as you are?"

"No, not really."

"I think that's half your battle."

"I think it's a battle I'll have for life."

"Aren't you tired of battling?"

"Knackered."

"So why don't you try and stop? Love yourself. Just as you are. Let others love you just as you are. Know that they love you."

"Sometimes I do wonder what the battle is for. It's my own doing. It could stop. If I had the guts."

"Have you?"

"I don't know."

"I think you have."

"Thanks."

"That's the truth. I think you have the guts. To stop running now. Face everything. Stop blaming yourself. Stop wanting to be punished. I think you have the guts for that."

"You have faith in me."

"And so does your new family. They have every faith in you."

"I'm so scared my real father will come back and ruin everything."

"If you have the guts to get better, you'll have the guts to know true love can't be ruined."

"You make it sound so simple."

"It's what you want to make it, Tanya. Simple or hard."

"I don't want to make it hard any more."

"Well, make that a promise to yourself. No one else can do it for you. The fight's yours."

"But it can be a simple fight?"

"Yes."

It made sense. Suddenly everything came miraculously together. I can do it. Me. Tanya Beecham.

"They'll help you, Tanya. Your family. Friends. But you have to help them by helping yourself. They can't do it all. It's down to you."

It's down to me. That was the simplicity of it. That was how simple. Me, who had been obsessed way down inside with the thought that I was nothing more than a walking monster. Now my future was in my hands. What had Chris said? Life is what you make it. And I'd said, well, what about if you don't make it? You die inside, that's what he'd said. You die inside. And what had that old man said at breakfast? Your one good eye could tell a whole different story. It's your character that matters. Your one good eye. Your character. Build that up and you're made.

Well, did I want to die? Really? Did I want to curl up and hide away? Did I want that? I wondered then. I could change it, you see. Everything. If what these different people had said was true, then I could make it. A new life. A fresh start. It could be made. I could learn to live with myself. Practice, the gentleman had said. Practice. Well, could I start? Now, to practise. Could I? Really?

"I don't think you'll be staying in this unit for long, Tanya. Ten days at the most. We'll review your drugs and see how you settle down. We'll give you your clothes back in a couple of days. Then you'll be able to go down to day hospital."

"OK."

"Another doctor will probably see you while you're in here but I'll see you before you leave. All right?"

"All right, thanks."

"OK, Tanya. I think you've got some visitors, so you'd better go and keep them company."

"All right."

"Bye, Tanya."

"Bye."

Chapter Twenty-Four

Mum and Gerry were waiting outside the doctor's office. I kissed them both and took them to my single room. Mum was loaded up. She'd brought me flowers, books, chocolates, writing paper, cards, prezzies, all wrapped up. It was like my birthday all over again.

"How come you're not at work, Mum?"

"Compassionate leave. I'll take a couple of days off."

"I'm much better. The doctor says I'll only have to stay in for about ten days."

"How're your wrists?" Mum asked.

"OK. Just a bit sore. I don't know when I'll have the stitches out."

"A few days' time, I expect," Gerry said. "Here you are. You've got some unwrapping to do." He laid the presents out on my bed. There were three of them.

"It's like my birthday."

"I'll go and find a vase for your flowers." Mum went off.

"Shall I open them now?"

"That's what they're for."

"I'll wait until Mum comes back."

"All right."

"You didn't have to buy me presents."

"We wanted to."

"I'm sorry about this, Gerry. I mean doing what I

did last night. I didn't mean to worry you both."

"Did you really want to die?"

"Everything was so terrible in my mind. I don't know."

"But now?"

"How long have I been ill for?"

"Since the accident, really."

"Two years?"

"About that."

"Why did they let me out of hospital then?"

"Because they couldn't do anything more for you at the time. Some things have to take their natural course."

"And now they have."

"It seems that way." He smiled. "But you have to make a go of it, Tanya. You have to keep going forward. One step at a time."

"It's all because you married Mum, isn't it? Why I got better."

"Things might have taken the same course anyway."

"You're too modest. I think it was because of you."

"Here's your Mum."

"Haven't you opened your presents yet?"

"She was waiting for you."

"Well, I'm here now."

I opened them. One was a nightie. Just the kind I like. Like a nightshirt. One was a pair of blue slippers and one was a book. Well, it felt like it from the outside. When I took the paper off there was a box inside. I opened the box and it was a leather-bound Bible. I was chuffed. Really chuffed. I mean, I'd never had my very own Bible before, not that I'd ever really wanted one. But if there was ever a time for me to have one then this was it. Gerry had written inside the cover. It was from him, Mum and the others. I kissed them both. For all the presents, but especially for the Bible.

They stayed about an hour and a half, chatting, and I showed them round the hospital. When they were leaving they told me that Sarah was coming in to see me that afternoon and they'd be back with the others in the evening. I hugged them both goodbye.

"All right, Tanya?" a male nurse asked when I'd seen them off.

"Yes, thanks."

"We're going to move your stuff to another room this afternoon."

"Oh, all right. My sister's coming in to see me this afternoon."

"That's good."

"They brought me a Bible."

"Did they? Are you religious?"

"I don't really know, actually."

He laughed. "Anyway, come down to the lounge. We could have a game of cards or something."

I went down to the lounge and had a game of cards with the nurse. Then he was called out, so I fetched one of the books Mum had brought in and read that until lunchtime.

I sat at the table with the same people I was with at breakfast. That woman kept staring at me again. It didn't really bother me then, though. She could stare as much as she wanted. That's the way I was feeling and it was a good way.

I lay on my bed after lunch. Just thinking. About

everything. I'd been so convinced I'd killed my sister. So convinced for such a long time. Now I knew I hadn't, that I wasn't an evil monster, well, I felt so much lighter inside. It was like a great boulder had been lifted from my shoulders. A great weight. I felt like someone again. A real person. I didn't feel twisted any more. Nothing was accusing me. Nothing. No one. Because I'd done no wrong.

They moved me to a larger room with four beds in it. I got chatting to another woman in there. She was in because of depression. I lent her one of my books, and then Sarah came in. We hugged each other.

"Here. You can get fat while you're in here." She gave me a box of chocolates.

"Thanks, Sarah. And for the card. Sit down."

"Am I allowed to sit on your bed?"

"Of course."

"How are you?"

"Fine."

"You look better. Your eye. Brighter, you know. Not clouded."

"Have you seen Chris?"

"I saw him last night. You told him, didn't you? Poor Chris was going round in circles. So was Robin until I told them the truth. You big nutcase, you."

"But I was thinking after lunch – Gerry shouted at me and he said he knew what I'd done."

"Yeah. That was all a big set-up. He wasn't really cross. He was putting all that on. We all were. Pretending to be cross with you. Conspiring with the doctors, you see. We wanted you to break. God, I was sweating it out in my bedroom. So was Dad. He felt awful for shouting at you. We were all just waiting. It was like a horror movie really. You see, the doctors knew you thought you killed your sister. But until you actually admitted it to someone it was no good. You had to come out with it yourself. They couldn't tell you."

"God. I can't think. It's all so damn confusing."

"Don't bother thinking. You're in here to rest, not to think."

"So, everyone knew."

"Yeah, and you were so damn stubborn. Keeping it to yourself all the time."

"I thought I'd be put in prison."

"You only thought you were a criminal because of the way you look."

That was the first time she'd ever actually mentioned anything about my scars. I felt embarrassed in a way.

She put her hand over mine. "We all love you, yer know. Just the way you are."

"Thanks."

"So, that's enough about that. At least you won't be in here very long. Not a bad place, though. I saw a dishy male nurse when I came in. With a moustache."

"Oh, that's Marc. I was playing cards with him earlier."

"All right for some. Hey, d'you think I can smoke in here?"

"I don't know. We could go down to the lounge. You can smoke in there."

"D'you want to, then?"

"Yeah, come on. Telly's on."

We went down to the lounge. She smoked. We talked. Watched telly. Had a cup of tea when the tea trolley came round.

"Chris is popping in after work. So he'll be in at about six. Then the others are coming at about seven."

"Chris? Really?"

"Of course."

"Oh no. I'll be embarrassed."

"Why?"

"Well. I will be."

"Don't be daft. He was so worried about you he has to come to convince himself that you're not dead."

I smiled at that.

"Anyway, I'd better be going, Tanya."

"You still working part-time?"

"Oh yeah. Dad's accepted it now."

"After the great row you had."

"We're too much alike, that's our trouble. Anyway, I'll pop in tomorrow afternoon. It'll do me good. All this cycling."

"OK. I'll walk to the door with you."

We kissed each other goodbye and she gave me a thumbs up before going.

Chapter Twenty-Five

I was getting in a right stew about Chris coming in to see me. I had the right jitters. I could hardly eat my dinner at five. Then I couldn't stay still. I was wandering around the unit, talking to a few people. I got so nervous that I even took a cigarette when a man offered me one.

At ten to six I combed my hair and cleaned my teeth. I didn't feel very respectable in my night clothes and dressing gown but after all I was in hospital. At least I was wearing my new slippers.

He was dead on time. I was sitting on my bed when a nurse brought him in. I stupidly blushed. Hoped he hadn't noticed. He had a bunch of flowers for me. Pink and white carnations. They were lovely. I pulled up a chair for him. After all my nerves, though, it was great to see him.

"I ought to tell you off," he said.

"Why?"

"You promised me you wouldn't do anything stupid."

"I'm sorry."

"I thought it was my fault."

"I'm sorry."

"It brought it all back about Mum. Dad was great, as usual. He managed to talk me out of my depression. When we found out the truth."

"Can you forgive me?"

"Thousands wouldn't, you know."

"But you're not thousands."

"I'll forgive you."

"Thank you."

"Anyway, how are you?"

"You helped me get better, Chris. I had to tell someone, you see. About me killing her. I had to tell someone. Just to get it out."

"Yeah. I've realized."

"I'm better, Chris. Everything, it's just wonderful."

"That pleases me. It really does. Dad sends his love, by the way. He says he's expecting to see you up at the club soon."

"Ten days. Or less."

"Have you seen your doctor?"

"Yeah. He was great. I'm really going to try now, Chris. Try. For everyone."

"That's what you have to do. Oh, I've got a card somewhere." He looked in his pockets. "Oh, here. From everyone at work. Mike said don't worry about your job. It'll still be waiting for you. Here."

I opened the card. It had a lovely verse inside and was signed by everyone at the shop. I put it with the rest of my cards.

"Everyone's been so lovely, Chris. Really they have."

"That's cause you're a lovely girl."

"Don't be daft."

"Well," he shrugged. "If you can't take a compliment."

"I'm embarrassed, that's all."

"Well, you shouldn't be."

"How did you get here?"

"Dad brought me. He's waiting outside. Cor, I passed a real nutty guy on my way up here. I thought he was going to punch me on the nose or something."

I laughed.

"It isn't funny. I've got to pass him again on the way down."

"We're all nutty in here."

"Especially you."

"Thanks."

We didn't speak for a while. It wasn't a tense kind of silence, though.

"Tanya?"

"Yeah."

"Will you go out with me?"

I was shocked. This was it. What happens. I'd never had a boyfriend before, you see. But this. This is what happens. In all those magazines I read. Girl and boy. Boy asks girl out. Girl says – Well, what should I say? What did I want to say?

"Yes." It was that simple.

"Pardon?"

"I said, yes. Of course I will."

He smiled. A lovely refreshing smile. Then he breathed a sigh of relief.

"You don't believe in keeping a guy waiting, do you?"

"Sorry."

"I'll be always having to forgive you, yer know. The amount of times you say sorry."

"Sorry." I was joking then.

"OK. So we're going out. Great. First date in hospital. What happens in this pad, babe?" He put on a voice. "Discos? Films?"

" 'Fraid not."

"Hey, I know what I've got. D'you want a fag?"

"I'm not sure if you're allowed to smoke in here."

"No one's around. We can use the flower-pot as an ashtray."

"OK."

"D'you want one."

"Just one then."

"It's a disgusting habit. I'm not forcing you."

"One day we'll give up together."

"Good idea. Here."

He lit both of our cigarettes.

"Has Sarah been in?"

"This afternoon."

"We didn't really feel like the disco last night, after all."

"My fault."

"Don't you dare say sorry."

I didn't say sorry.

The hour passed too quickly. Chris wanted to leave before my family arrived. I think he was feeling a bit shy really. I walked with him down to the door and he said he'd be in to see me the next day.

"You be good," he said.

"I always am."

"No flirting with your doctor."

"God, he's about fifty."

"I thought you might like older men."

"I like you." I felt embarrassed. The words had just sort of popped out. He kissed me then. On the lips. It wasn't a long kiss but it was beautiful. His mouth tasted lovely.

"See yer, Tanya."

"Take care."
"Bye."

I was beaming when I walked back to my bedroom. I felt ten foot tall. I've got a boyfriend. I've got a boyfriend. I've got a boyfriend. It was an elating feeling. I couldn't wait until Mum and Gerry came so that I could tell them. My first ever boyfriend.

I lay on my bed. Looked at all the flowers around me. All the cards. It's all happened, I thought. It's all happened and I've survived it. I've come through. I've come through. And I could feel so much love inside me. So much warmth. Something I never realized I had.

Monsters are cold.

I knew then that I wasn't a monster. I knew then that I could love and be loved. Because everyone had proved it to me. It didn't matter what I looked like. I could survive. As long as I could love I knew I could survive. And that's all I wanted to know just then. That's all I needed to know. Everything else could go to hell.

Everything else could go to hell.

I knew love didn't belong there.

I finally knew I didn't belong there.

Other Faber Teenage Paperbacks

THE ROOM WITH NO WINDOWS
Gene Kemp

'Everything here is out of this world, though I'm not sure
I fit in. Sometimes I feel as if I'm a raw onion being
peeled, layer by layer till there's nothing left, especially if
Harry picks on me. Sometimes I've got things to say but
I'm scared to, for if I do, it sounds false or funny, peculiar
not ha-ha, or someone else says something wittier or
louder or cleverer and nobody hears me. But it doesn't
matter because I can talk to Tass.'

Gene Kemp's third novel for teenagers describes a young
girl's emotional turmoil as the holiday of a lifetime
gradually turns into a nightmare . . .

'Kemp remains a first-rate storyteller.' Naomi Lewis,
Observer

0–571–16117–0

JOSEPHINE
Kenneth Lillington

'Josephine Tugnutt was excusably nervous as she walked up the tree-lined avenue that led to St Chauvin's College. One girl among six hundred boys! She came from a girls' boarding school, and was walking into the unknown . . .'

It's 1932, the year of the great Yo-Yo craze, and St Chauvin's is another world altogether. What strikes Josephine as odd at first glance, appears even more so at a second. Why does the English master make such free play with his sword? Did the science master really turn a boy into a wolf? Is Fearless of the Fifth quite what he would wish one to believe? With a no-nonsense thoroughness that does not, however, rule out the possibility of romance, Josephine sets about putting things to rights — with hilarious results.

'A frothy, sophisticated treat.' Stephanie Nettell, *Guardian*

0-571-16118-9

ALMOST JAPANESE
Sarah Sheard

'Everything Japanese was magic. Sheepskin coats were magic. I'd spot a car like his and my heart would jump. In the grocery store, I heard a laugh just like his and I almost died. Everything that connected to him was absolutely sacred. My daily life was so ordinary it was painful.'

Emma is fourteen when she meets and falls hopelessly in love with the distinguished Japanese musician, Akira Tsutsuma. The problems caused by the age difference between her and Akira and the objections of her parents finally put an end to her obsession for a man, but not her love of life and all things Japanese.

'An exquisitely crafted story.' *The Times*

'A real find.' *Look Now*

0-571-14863-8

FAMILY FEELING
Gina Wilson

Families can be difficult even when they are your own.
When they are not really your own they can be worse.

Alice Mather was thirteen when her widowed mother
married Donald Spenser. He was divorced; his daughter
Corinna was eight and his son Edwin fifteen. Corinna did
not like her stepmother but she took to Alice – as long
as Alice indulged her. The smallest sign of neglect and
she would do her best to make trouble. As to Edwin, he
hardly looked at Alice at first; but it was different
later . . .

Gina Wilson is an exceptional writer for teenagers, and
Family Feeling is both a dramatic account of dangerous
shifts in family relationships and the story of tentative
first love. All her novels for young people show her
penetrating but sympathetic insight into teenage
emotions.

0–571–16119–7